ONE FRIGHT ONLY

Patrick Tumblety

UNCOMFORTABLY DARK HORROR

"Tumblety knows what makes a great slasher. One Fright Only wraps a murder mystery and con- spiracy thriller around a masked killer, all with- out relying on the same tropes that have made modern slashers feel played out. His characters are multifaceted, and the story really captures that Halloween atmosphere. Highly recommend- ed!"— Elford Alley, author of APARTMENT 239 and NEVER LEAVING

DEDICATION

For Dad

You taught me one of the most important life lessons:

When no door is available, make one.

The doors open; screams escape from inside.
It's Halloween again, and you are next in line…

BADGER FARMS

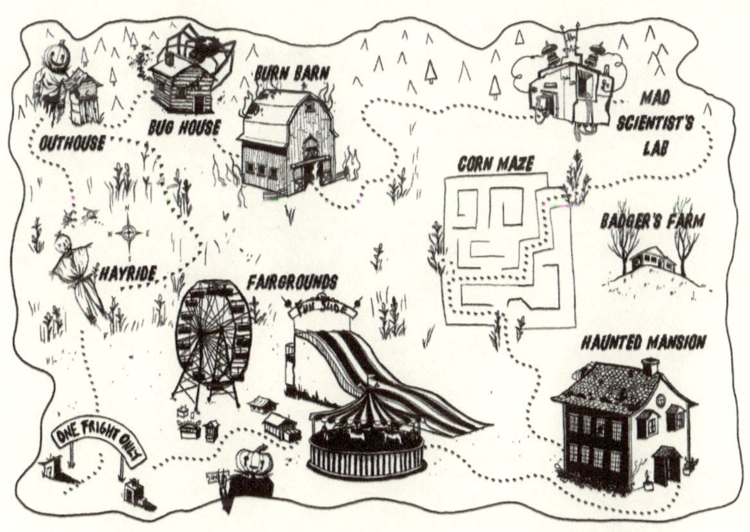

ONE FRIGHT ONLY HAUNTED ATTRACTION

PROLOGUE

SUNDAY, OCTOBER 26TH

ELISE DOESN'T UNDERSTAND THE appeal of Halloween.

As a kid, she rolled her eyes at rubber-masked teens jumping out of closets and plastic spiders dangling on strings. Her cousins used a Ouija board to scare her during a sleepover when she was twelve, and she pretended to be scared to keep them from insisting that she was "just trying to play it cool." Her sorority made freshmen sleep in a cemetery overnight for initiation. The lameness almost forced her to revoke her pledge. Nothing about Halloween, from scary movies to creepy crawlies, ever created a single goosebump on her skin.

The monstrous house in front of her is no exception, especially since she had a hand in building it, or rather, tearing it apart to look disheveled. She had splattered the back of the three-story ranch house with red paint, dirtied the carpets, and hammered holes in the plaster. She'd glued spider webs across the interior walls and splashed neon paint across a few others. Had she been able to time-travel to tell her younger self she would be working at a haunted house attraction; she is sure that bratty little girl would have called her "lame."

No, the house doesn't scare her, even now that the last of twilight had given way to darkness... but there is a reason she did not volunteer to work in the corn maze.

She turns around to stare at the fairgrounds. The innocent jolliness of the carousel and the cartoon characters hanging from game booths as prizes seemed to be oppressed by the surrounding crop. No way to rise above the stalks. No way to see through them. A natural prison. She reaches into her jeans to pull out a pack of nicotine gum but finds it empty.

An electrical boom destroys the quiet night and forces her body to twitch. One of the fifty-foot-tall floodlights rising from within the crop switches off, darkening a section of the farm and the fairground attractions. Although she knows the next floodlight is about to follow suit, her body still reacts at the sound. The "Undead Carousel" falls to the darkness, followed by the concession stands as the next light dims off. One by one, the floodlights that semicircle the grounds die until she is alone with only a hint of illumination from the moon.

It's okay, she thinks. *Darkness is a good thing. He won't be able to see me.*

Gabe, her boyfriend, is responsible for turning off the lights when the staff goes home, which means he will be heading to his car. She had kissed him goodbye and driven away before backtracking and parking at the side entrance so he wouldn't see her car when he left for the night. Without him here, her craving for a cigarette rises, and she doesn't know if it's because she can have one guilt-free when he's not around, or if doing two things that he has asked her to stop doing will make her feel more independent.

This isn't about him, Elise reminds herself.

The porch light above the door blinks to life, welcoming her inside. Her stomach clenches, and something lower in her body stirs. She opens the door and steps inside. The musk of the haunted house greets her at the entrance. Plastic, paint, machinery—phantoms of the attraction.

"Babe?" She closes the door and yells. Her voice returns to the atrium from its travel through the dark corridors.

The chandelier above the atrium bursts to life, illuminating a face staring at her from a foot away. She screams and then steps backward until her back hits the door. Her eyes adjust to the light enough for her to realize the face is too pale to be human, and she remembers the plastic skeleton she tied to the post at the bottom of the circular staircase that leads to the second floor.

She laughs, trying to fight off the atypical nervousness.

"Where are you?" she yells. An answer arrives alongside her echo as another light switches on from beyond the second-floor balcony.

"Cute," she grumbles, but cracks a smile.

The stairs creak as she ascends to the second floor. Thick webbing stretches across the atrium's walls and rises towards "Her Majesty" as she stretches her eight legs across the domed ceiling. Each room in the house has a "Premier Scare." In the atrium, the Spider Queen reigns. The moving spotlights on a track behind the spider cast thick shadows around the room, a dizzying effect that instills the feeling of spiraling into a web.

She admires John, the attraction's creator, for his creativity. She smiles at the memory of him on top of her. Inside of her.

At the top of the staircase, a strobing purple light greets her from the end of the adjacent hall. The darkness between the bursts of light reveals splattered neon paint across the walls and floor. A hidden door is in the left wall, where one of the actors will emerge to scare their victims. Black strings hang from the ceiling, creating a feeling of bugs brushing across faces. A "Scare Umbilical," as John calls all hallways. "Pregnant with frights that hint at the theme of the next room."

She assumes she is being led toward the room at the back of the house, where a clown lit by lights on its costume will await its victims. There will be no room light, so there is no need for a camera. She appreciates the secrecy, is tantalized by it, but she would rather get down to business than deal with theatrics.

The strobing is disorienting, so she places a hand on the wall for support as she follows the neon splatter across the floor. The next burst of light is cut off as someone crosses its source.

She is about to call out when she feels a hand grab her wrist. She tries to fight but is pulled toward the sliding trapdoor in the wall at shoulder height in the middle of the hallway. An arm wraps around her chest, and she is lifted through the opening. Despite knowing this is a prank, she screams as the bottom of the wooden opening scrapes against her back and burns her skin. She drops onto the wooden floor, and the collision sends a ripple of pain through her body.

"That fucking hurt," she says as she places her hand on her back while she sits up. She looks up to see her lover dropping inside the room from the trap door wearing that year's crew costume, an orange oval mask with spray-painted, dripping black eyes and a thick, dark brown robe.

"Funny," she winces through the lingering pain and raises a hand. "Help me up."

The pumpkin's hand passes hers to reach into the robe's pocket on the other side.

"Don't be a cunt," Elise says and shakes her hand.

The pumpkin pulls a metal object from its robe. Elise can't tell in the low light if it's a knife or a garden trowel, but its rough exterior tells her it is caked with rust.

"I'm not in the mood for anything rough tonight," she shakes her hand again, "but if you play your cards right-"

The rusted metal glides through the air, scraping across her palm and opening her skin, deep enough to carry blood on the blade and splatter it across the wall. Elise screams and recoils towards the wall, and the pumpkin follows.

"What the fuck?" she yells as she uses her other hand to stand. The pumpkin grabs a handful of her hair and slams her head violently against the wall. The side of her head hits the wood and jostles her brain, dizzying her thoughts and vision.

"What are you...?" A sensation she has never felt before erupts in her abdominal muscles. Her breath and attention are so taken with this odd feeling that she does not even have the wherewithal to scream. Instead, her fight-or-flight response takes over, and she chooses both. She pushes off the wall, into the attacker's shoulder, knocking them out of the way of the trapdoor. She moves towards it but stops as her stomach erupts in pain.

The weapon slides out of her body and splatters blood across the floor. She pushes against the bloody opening in her shirt and fights against the pain as she adds pressure to the wound. Her other hand slides the trapdoor upwards, and she leans into the chest-high ledge, bearing the pain of it digging into her ribs as she lets her body tilt and drop into the neon hallway. She hits the ground, and the pain elicits the loudest scream she has ever unleashed.

Her legs shake enough to keep her from standing upright, so she uses one hand to balance on the wall and the other to apply pressure to the wound, which also helps to close the wound on her palm. Hearing the trapdoor slide open helps her fight through the pain and hurry down the hallway toward the atrium. One of her shoes drops from her foot, but instead of going back for it, she kicks off the other and slides on her socks towards the second-floor railing. She risks a glance backward to see her pursuer climbing out of the trapdoor, then leans against the railing to half slide, half skip down the steps.

"Who the fuck are you?" she screams, and the outburst nearly depletes her remaining energy. The moving shadows from the spider's webbing threaten her balance, but she manages to reach the atrium floor without falling. She tries to place weight on her right side, but the pain is too much, so she hops towards the front door, taking another glance towards the steps to see her attacker quickening their descent.

Her body tells her that she can't keep moving for much longer, so she steps outside and uses her remaining strength to cross the field toward the carousel. If she can make it, there are hidden spaces to hide under the rides and inside the gaming booths. She reaches the floor of the carousel and rolls onto it. Crouched, she shimmies under the horses and around the central hub that houses the ride's mechanics until she is on the other side.

From there, she heads straight towards the first booth she sees; a roulette wheel with rubber duckies and dolphin stuffies for prizes. She is too weak to lift herself over the booth, so she moves around the side and through the hinged half-door of the staff entrance, staying low and ducking under the front counter.

The pain and blood loss rush into her now that she is lying still, but the adrenaline keeps her alert. She hears dirt crunch on the other side of the booth, so she steadies her breathing to stay as silent as her body will allow.

Questions about the person's identity begin to seep in along with the fatigue, and her reasoning behind why she is being attacked terrifies her more than the current moment. Only one of two people could be behind that mask, and even if Gabe did find out about her transgressions, he didn't have the personality or capability for violence. The only reason she is being attacked is that someone knew she was going to confess to the police about the plan... but she only told two people, and neither of them would betray her trust.

A loud bang erupts against her ear and forces her to scream. The masked attacker jumps onto the bar top and kneels, looking down at Elise before swinging the blade downward in an arc. Elise rolls out from under it just in time and then hurls her body towards the hinged door. With her attacker too close for her to hide, her only option is to weave through the booths and rides to reach the crop. The muscles in her wounded side clench, and her leg seizes, forcing her to hop the rest of the way into the cornstalks.

After a few yards, she pivots left, trying not to rustle the dried leaves or crunch them underfoot, hoping to lose her attacker and circumvent around to the hayride trail so she can backtrack to her car. Her side finally gives out and sends her to the ground, crunching dried stalks and kicking up dirt.

She listens for movement while sliding her muddy socks off her feet. The tops of a few stalks wave from several yards away, giving her another reason to hate this graveyard of dried husks. If she moves, their sway will give up her position, but at least they let her know where the other person is as well, never having considered that the same fear of being inside a cornfield might also save her life. She sees the robe's dark form enter the nearest dirt path between the rows. The pumpkin looks around, and its confusion fills her with hope.

Turn away. Don't head this way.

She sees the pumpkin looking down at the nearest stalk, where a wet patch glistens under the moonlight. She looks at her bloody hand and clothes, and then up at the stalk she is hiding under, painted with her blood. The mask looks up and follows the blood trail towards her position. She wants to slink away, but knows that if she moves, she will be detected. As unflinching as her aching body will allow, she waits and hopes.

Her weight shifts lower to the ground, cracking the bedding of dried stalks beneath her and sending a *crack* into the night.

The dark, splattered eyes of the pumpkin's bright, seemingly disembodied head turn towards her. She pushes onto her feet and flees as fast as her perforated body will allow, pivoting in and out of adjacent rows in hopes of confusing...

But who is attacking her?

The thought is fleeting as she collides face-first with a hard object. Several teeth crack, a rib breaks, and when her body hits the ground, she knows it will never get up.

The moon, the canopy of stalks, and the burlap head of the scarecrow, whose post she collided with, spin wildly as her mind spirals towards unconsciousness. The pumpkin walks into her view and hovers above. It kneels and reaches out a hand to caress her face, fingers tracing from behind her ear, down her jawline, and ending at the tip of her chin. The sensual movement is specific, telling her that despite the mask, she knows exactly why she is in this moment.

"I told you I won't tell," she cries as hard as she is able. "I want to do this with you. Be with you. Let me prove it to you." She reaches out her arms towards her attacker.

The pumpkin mask stares at her without moving, and Elise feels relief that her ruse is working. Her attacker walks a few steps away and stops by the scarecrow's post, so she digs her heels into the dirt to get ready to push to her feet and run.

The pumpkin pulls out its weapon again and grabs the rope that ties the scarecrow to the cross. Elise pushes against the dirt but knows she will not escape what is about to happen. The attacker cuts the rope, and the scarecrow falls forward. Elise's final thought is of the face behind the mask, and how they have betrayed each other.

Her heart breaks just before her skull cracks.

Chapter 1

Monday, October 27th

A GUM WRAPPER ROLLS across a dirt path that separates two rows of dried cornstalks. David plucks it from the ground and recognizes the brand name of nicotine gum. He unclips the walkie-talkie from his jeans and presses the call button. Nearly two dozen walkies squelch across the ten-acre land like squawking crows.

"Anyone on?"

"I'm here," John Lowenstein's strained voice replies. David thinks about what he is going to say because John is the creator and head engineer of the attraction. Other than the farmland's owner, Lillian, he is in charge. He presses the call button.

"I'm walking in for the day and don't see Elise. She's not with Earnest." He looks up at the wooden cross towering above the canopy, its twisted branches vacant of the hay-stuffed scarecrow with a burlap head. "Neither is Earnest." He releases the button and waits.

"Lillian says Elise didn't check in. Earnest probably fell. Fix it."

"Roger," David says, and then winces. The walkie-talkie squelches and laughter distorts through the speaker.

"Geek," a young man's voice teases, belonging to any of the senior workers.

"Get off the channel, Mark," John says, emphasizing the young man's name.

David clips the walkie back onto his belt, straining the fraying leather. He doesn't have a backup, so he will have to add a new belt to the list of growing items he needs to purchase when he gets his final paycheck of the season.

Pieces of stalks and dried corn crunch under his feet, and bugs fly into his face. The afternoon sun is unusually warm for this late in October, so he stops to take off his flannel button-down and tie it around his waist. His foot hits something solid but pliable, the arm of a tattered grey suit jacket with hay jutting out from its tears and cuffs. His feet dig into the mud around the scarecrow as he pulls on the jacket's collar. The burlap sack face pops out of the ground and falls back into the mud. The hay's wetness makes it heavier than it looks. David pulls the radio from his belt and regrets what he is about to ask.

"The scarecrow is too heavy. I need some help."

"It's hay," a voice laughs that sounds like Mark's again, but deeper. Mark's twin, Kevin.

"I'll go," a woman's voice volunteers. David's heart beats faster.

A different male voice follows, most likely Ryan's. "Oooh," he taunts.

"Fuck off, Ryan," scolds the woman.

"From now on," John cuts through, "this channel is only for work."

David can still hear laughter from beyond the stalks. The closest anyone can be where they can still hear is in the Outhouse, Mark's station.

"They are just little boys," Kyra says over the radio, "they can't help it."

The laughter over the stalks dies.

David clips the walkie-talkie then runs a hand through his curly hair. He straightens his shirt and reties his flannel. He inhales the crisp autumn air and releases it slowly, ending as he hears Kyra's footsteps crunch along the field only a few feet away. He watches the tops of the stalks sway as she draws closer, and although he has seen her every day for over a month, he cannot help but physically react to her attractiveness as she steps into the barren circle around the base of the cross.

Kyra's aesthetic makes her both a part of the environment and nothing like it. Her black hair, normally waist-length, is pulled up into a messy bun, and her pale skin is burned from working weeks in the sun. Her black tank top and blue jeans show tattoos across both arms. A cat silhouette in the middle of intricate, flowing line work on one, and a dagger through a heart in the middle of maze-like angles on the other. She is petite, but muscular. A Goth girl who got into farming, or a farm girl who never gave up Goth. The other seniors treat her with the same reverence as a crow regards a scarecrow, a healthy mix of awe and fear.

"Hey, Shaggy." She smiles, calling back to a conversation they shared a week ago. He discovered her and another senior worker, Pam, sharing a joint in the parking area after work. She commented on his curly hair and flannel button-down shirt, and how they made him look like a stoner straight out of the late nineties. An observation he had to refute when he declined to take a hit of the joint.

"Hey, Velma," he says.

"Velma?" She places a hand on her sternum to feign offense. "I thought I was Daphne?"

"No," David recalls. He remembers having to fumble for words to reply to her observation. He thought she was making fun of him, but then she said she "dug" it, and kept talking. He doesn't know what it's like to be high but assumes she either doesn't remember his contribution to the conversation because of that, or because he isn't memorable.

"You said people think you're *'all looks'* like Daphne, but you have Velma's nerdy heart."

"So, you don't think I have the looks?"

David's face flushes. "I fell right into that, didn't I?" Embarrassed, yes, but at least she remembered the conversation he had thought about for the rest of the night...and ever since.

"Yes, you did," Kyra laughs. "Let's get Earnest back on his feet."

"His cross, you mean," David says.

"His cross. The symbol of our Jersey-born religion." She leans forward to grab one side of Earnest's jacket. The collar of her shirt hangs down far enough for David to see more of her chest than he might be allowed. He also notices the head of a black snake tattoo rising from her back and resting on her shoulder, its tongue licking the air. He turns his face away and steps over Earnest to lift the other side.

"Nothing like things falling apart during the last week of rehearsal," he says.

"That's right, you did theater work in high school." Besides Lillian and John, Kyra was the only other person present during his job interview.

"I did backstage work for the community theater after high school." David catches his words, not wanting to seem younger than he is. "I'm in college now. Or rather, I would be, but I'm taking a year off." He begs himself to stop talking.

"This week is the most fun around here. You going to the party Wednesday night?"

"I didn't know there was a party," he strains to say as they lift Earnest's chest.

"Of course," Kyra rolls her eyes, "they didn't tell you. The Wednesday before opening night, we have a party. Everyone is invited, but the..." she seethes as she says, "senior workers here like to leave the newbies out." By seniors, he knows she doesn't mean "old", like the carnival workers or the construction staff, but the group of people she graduated with who haven't moved out of town to pursue higher education or employment. They are the production staff working directly under John's management and Kyra's supervision.

"They won't mind if I come?" David asks, with the subtext of the question being, *Will I be the subject of bullying and ridicule?*

"I won't mind," Kyra says with a stern face. "John and Lillian might be in charge, but I run this place. Think of me as the stage manager of a play. If any of these adolescents want to come back next year, they won't care who I invite to the party."

"Okay," David says, trying to hide his excitement. "I'll be there."

They strain to hold Earnest upright as Kyra pulls a rope from underneath its collar and throws it in a loop over the highest post. She motions for David to grab his side of the rope, and together they hoist the body onto the cross.

"The rain makes the hay into a whole other substance," she says as they pull.

"It hasn't rained in a while," he says.

"It probably fell when it rained last weekend and trapped the moisture beneath."

He is not about to argue with her, even though he saw it up there on his way out last night.

"Can you hold it yourself?" she asks and offers him her side of the rope. David takes it and pulls on both sides, holding Earnest aloft while Kyra uses the ropes around its chest and arms to tie it down.

"You're stronger than you look, Shaggy."

"Thanks," he says, trying to play the compliment off like his arms are not about to be pulled out of their sockets. She finishes tying the rope and nods for him to let go. Earnest stands high once again. Kyra takes out a pocketknife, pulls the blade out of its sheath with her teeth, then cuts the end of the rope that hangs from the knot.

"Thanks for letting us know about poor Earnest here." She pockets the knife then places her hands on her hips to bend her back until it cracks.

"Ouch," David says.

"Twenty-four going on forty," she says. "That's what you get when you trade a college desk for farm life."

"How long have you been doing this?"

"About five years, but it's not just for the season. The Badgers are family friends. Lillian used to babysit me. When I decided to stay in the area and attend virtual college, they hired me to help with the farm. Been here since I was your age."

Embarrassment, again, takes hold. He is only five years younger, but to someone going through their senior year of college, a high-school graduate must seem like a child.

"Thanks for your help," David says.

"No, thank you, Shaggy." She turns and pushes a stalk out of her way but stops and turns back. "Can I ask you something personal?"

"Sure," he says, happy to have her stay.

"Has anyone bothered you about...?" she trails off.

"I don't think they've put it together," he says. "But in a town this small..." he shrugs.

"Let me know if they do," she says. "Although they aren't that bright, so..." She mimics his shrug and smiles before disappearing into the stalks.

David holds back a lump in his throat. Those were the nicest words anyone has said to him in almost a year. The walkie-talkie squawks, and Kyra says, "David handled it on his own." Which is the nicest thing anyone has done for him in almost a year.

Queen of the Crows, he thinks.

He walks under Earnest and nearly slips on the mud. He scrapes the sole of his sneaker against a downed stalk and then checks the bottom to see if he got it all. The white sole has been tinted red, possibly from something in the mud. After giving both soles a few more scrapes, he walks toward the dirt path. David leaves the corn and heads through the attraction's entrance, travels between the closed gate and the ticket booth, and enters a service building that has been converted into the attraction's communications house.

At one point in the farm's history, a baseball diamond lay where the carnival rides reside. The building used to be a food shack where the farm cooked hot dogs, brewed tea, and served apple cider during games, or when the farm hosted apple, orange, and berry-picking year-round. That was so long ago that even David's father didn't remember attending the games when he was younger. The counter is stained, and rust covers a deep sink and a grill, which has been covered with a thick cut of wood to turn it into a desk.

John and Lillian lean on a table in the main kitchen area. Lillian points her finger at John, anger emanating from her eyes.

"The insurance on the pyrotechnics alone is insane," Lillian spits at him.

"What did you want me to do, decline it?" John sighs.

David has noticed the friction between them since his interview. Lillian asked what he would do if given conflicting orders, since he might have two bosses. He tried not to freeze under the pressure, then thought about his father's stories about workplace problems. He remembered a story about the leader of his father's corporate office arguing with the leader of his local office.

His father explained: "I ended up responding on the same email and telling them a third way of doing things that was beyond ridiculous. Both told me as much and then agreed on a solution. Let them handle their business and don't be anyone's puppet." David remembered that story and responded with humor, "No matter which person I listen to, I'm making someone angry, so I would lock you both in the haunted maze until you came up with one solution or at least put you on one email reply and let you decide." They laughed, commented that it was a good answer, and the interview continued.

John catches David walking across the room.

"Thanks for the help with Earnest," he says, "but you were late."

David tries to defend himself but is interrupted by Lillian.

"David and his mother share one car," she explains. "He was very clear about his arrival time when we hired him." John's eyes shift towards Lillian to send her nothing but a look of contempt, but then he nods at David.

"I forgot, I'm sorry."

"It's tech week," David shrugs, lifting his hands in the air.

"It *is* tech week," John laughs.

David walks towards the back room and catches Lillian's eye. She nods at him, and he mouths *"thank you."* He hates that people tiptoe around him and wonders if, had John and Lillian not been desperate for a last-minute replacement, he would have been rejected due to what has been revealed about his father in the past year.

The man he is replacing, Gabe Fowler, stands in the center of the media room, aglow in the artificial light from the desk of five monitors, making him look like a projection instead of a person. He speaks into a walkie, "Tap it to see if there's a wire loose."

Two CRT box monitors set on top of each other bookend a wide, flat monitor on the desk. Gabe said the flat screen was his addition after he saw how antiquated the monitors were when he started working at the farm five years ago. A dark-haired man with sideburns fills the screen of the left CRT, Ryan, one of the seniors. His breath fogs up the camera, and static fills the screen with each tap.

"I'll replace it," Gabe sighs into the walkie. Ryan backs away and waves before moving out of frame, leaving a screen of stalks that make up the walls of the corn maze.

"Is it necessary?" Lillian's voice calls from the other room.

Gabe never raises his voice above a decibel, so he answers with the walkie-talkie.

"Yes," he says.

"Can you tell me why?" Lillian yells.

Gabe looks away from the monitor and shakes his head. David raises his hand to stop Gabe from answering and then unclips his walkie, knowing Lillian won't argue with him.

"It's David. Gabe is fixing something," he lies. "Hundreds of people are going to be stomping through the maze. All we will get is static."

Lillian's sigh carries from the other room.

"Gabe has the account number," she relents. "Send him to the store so we don't risk shipping delays. Remind me to give you the number before you leave tonight."

David almost says "Roger" again but stops himself.

"Okay."

"Don't you mean, 'Roger?'" Mark's voice calls through the radio. Pam laughs in the background.

"I checked all the connections," Gabe says, "but I want to do a live feed test when we do our run-through tomorrow morning." He lifts the radio again and clicks the button. "I'm leaving to buy a new camera." He places the walkie-talkie in one of the many empty charging stations in the room.

"What do you want me to do while you're out?" David asks.

"Run through the other cameras and call me if you think of any other supplies we might need. I trust you."

"Thanks, man," David says, but Gabe is already out of the room. His compliment gives David a much-needed ego boost. Gabe is resigning because he has been offered a production position at a multimedia agency in Los Angeles and will be leaving for there tomorrow, having been unable to move the start date by a week to finish out the season.

David was hired as Gabe's replacement and has been working under the man for a month to ensure he is up to speed, and he suspects that John and Lillian are grooming him to be the new Gabe for the next several years. If he can afford to, he hopes to be well underway with college and away from New Jersey sooner rather than later, hopefully studying film in LA or New York, so he can remain closer to home.

During his interview, John mentioned that he and Gabe were impressed with his film reel and couldn't believe that the work he created was from high-school projects. David didn't consider them notable: a couple of social media setups for a guy he met who wanted to make money streaming, still photography for a local dance studio, a behind-the-scenes style documentary for a local youth choir that was competing in a national competition, and a few editing pieces where he re-created movie trailers to change the genre they were advertising.

"It shows you have skill with a variety of cameras, technology, and streaming, which is exactly what we need," John had said. This year, for the first time in the farm's twelve-year history, they will live-stream the scares online through their website.

He plops into the desk's ripped-leather recliner and presses a button on a switchboard in front of the monitors. The image on one of the left CRT monitors splits into four frames, one image of the grounds and the other three showing corn stalks that make up the walls of the walk-through maze. The monitor it sits on top of shows a wide view of the ticket and fairgrounds beyond from the camera mounted on the event sign above the main entrance.

The eight frames displayed on the flat screen show the main feed inside each attraction. He presses a button on the switchboard to fill the screen with the first image: a dilapidated porch on the side of a forest pathway. From its awning hangs the skin of an animal and a fake human corpse. He's not sure what will happen in that attraction but hopes to find out if he gets the opportunity to take a ride.

A patch of red crosses one of the two windows. He pulls out his phone and texts, *"I see you. Good morning."* He does not receive a text response but instead hears the front door of the facade burst open. A woman with wild, orange-red curls runs from the open doorway, down the stairs, and towards the camera, screaming, "Good morning, David!"

Tracy was his best friend, and the person who told him that the position was open. She had been attending community college since graduating from high school, and this is her second year working for the attraction. He smiles and texts her a laughing emoji. She pulls the phone from her jeans, sees the text, then offers a smile and a middle finger to the camera before walking up the stairs.

David clicks the button for the next image and sees the interior of a barn, filled with hay bales and looking ordinary. He hasn't seen any of this year's attractions live, so he doesn't know what this scare is supposed to be, but every previous year, the barn has been his favorite. If he stays with this job, he has a ton of new ideas that would make the barn creepy, if John lets him propose ideas. This year, the attraction is called the "Burn Barn", although he has no context for what that means.

The next image is black. He assumes it's supposed to be a view of the Mad Scientist's Laboratory because Gabe told him he hasn't installed that camera. The following image is a floor-to-ceiling shot of the haunted house's atrium, covered in webs with a giant spider hanging from the roof.

He clicks through the remaining three images, each from a different part of the haunted house. The mummy museum on the main floor, where the mummies come to life, and a room in the back that is decorated to look like a jungle growing from the walls and floor, with dinosaur masks that pop out of the foliage. The last of the house's cameras pans through a neon-lit hallway on the second floor. A section of the opposite wall is made to drop, unleashing a pumpkin-headed staff member that will pop out and reach for patrons. That hallway leads to a room of neon-lit clowns too dark to set a camera.

The hallway camera pans from the left wall to the right, and back again. David sees an object on the floor at the back of the hallway, where a purple light will strobe and disorient visitors. A mouse or a bird, maybe. He lifts his walkie-talkie and clicks the button.

"Dougie, are you at your post? I think a bird is in the hallway." He clicks a button on the monitor to turn up the contrast, revealing that the small object is a neon-pink sneaker, not a bird. He takes his cell phone out of his pocket and texts Dougie.

Don't answer the walkie-talkie if you heard it. I'm dumb.

Three dots show on the phone indicating that Dougie is replying.

No worries. I was in the bathroom. BRT

Relieved, he turns his attention back to the shoe. Only Elise wears neon-pink sneakers. Why her shoe is there, he doesn't know.

A pale hand reaches out from around the corner and snatches the shoe away. David waits to see if Elise walks into view, but the hallway remains abandoned until Dougie enters from the bottom of the screen, then turns to look up at the camera and wave. David smiles and looks at the right CRT monitors, which show views from the north and east sides of the fairground, bustling with workers of all ages, testing the rides and prepping the booths.

A crew member places logs and stones around two spots at the center of the grounds to create large bonfires where visitors can eat, drink, and roast marshmallows. Another crew sets up stacks of jack-o'-lanterns made and donated by kids in the elementary schools across town to be lit and placed around the entrance like otherworldly greeters. The slight curve and low resolution create the illusion of watching a low-budget horror movie, and he cannot be happier, because this will be the closest opportunity he has had to make something like that.

Sadness overtakes him as he remembers late nights watching scary movies with his father, riding the hayride, and drinking hot apple cider sitting by the bonfires every Halloween, every year he can remember. He spins his chair away from the monitors and stares into the darkness, willing his thoughts not to snowball and send him into a depressive state.

He still doesn't know if taking this job is a good idea, but he won't know until it's over. For now, he needs to concentrate on earning money, regardless of how he feels about his situation. His family needs him to step up in his father's absence.

David spends the rest of the day setting up the hardline for the Ethernet and the connections for the Wi-Fi and modem. The plan is to test the website's streaming at home that night to ensure anyone can log on and watch without interference. He also installs a mirroring program on his laptop so he can check the cameras from home and check out the grounds if he's feeling extra nostalgic or trying to impress his mother and brother.

Normal chatter squawks through the walkies, and some of the senior staff walk in to switch theirs out for freshly charged ones. Towards the end of the day, John performs his checks around the farm, from the senior staff, the fairground engineers and operators, and the special effects handlers for the main attractions.

"How are communications looking?" he asks.

"We look good," David answers.

"Great," John says with a stress-laden sigh.

"I'll run it with Gabe again tomorrow, but I think we're ready."

"I totally had faith in the new guy," Ryan chimes in.

"There's one thing left to do," John says. "David, you're the closest. Will you do the honor?"

His heart races. He knows exactly what John is referring to and is grateful for the opportunity. "Roger," he says, not caring if he will be ridiculed.

He walks outside and exits the main gate. Dusk bathes the field in pink and orange. The tops of the haunted attractions peak out from below the canopies, and the timed lights of the countless jack-o'-lanterns around the farm blaze to life. He breathes in the smell of burning wood and revels in the chilly autumn air.

This is what I needed, he thinks. After the year he had, he never thought he would feel this alive again. He looks up at the sign; hundreds of tiny bulbs are inlaid into a wooden frame.

"Ready," he says into the walkie-talkie.

John speaks through radio, "I officially want to thank you all for your hard work. I already know this will be our scariest, most successful year."

He hopes. Tickets usually sell out in August when they go on sale, but this year there are still a few hundred left. The farm used to be one of the most popular Halloween attractions in the Tri-State area, but extreme haunts and virtual reality experiences have been pulling people away from handmade, homegrown events. This is the first year that the attraction has not run every weekend in October, an indication of its dwindling sales.

But John is an incredible designer and engineer. He can pull it off if enough people see his creations, which David assumes is the reason for the live feed.

"Watch people get terrified live online!"

"Thank you to Lillian, as always, for her land and time. Kyra for her incredible leadership, and Gabe and David for opening a new window to our online future. David, I turned on the breaker, so if you will, do us the honor?"

Excitement surges through him. This kind of rush is exactly why he wanted to work at the attraction. He walks over to the right side of the sign and reaches around a metal post to find the switch. He does not need to be told where it is because he discovered it while standing in line when he was twelve. He flips it, and the green bulbs light up the darkening sky. Screams of joy ring out over the crops and rides; the crew whooping and hollering with excitement and anticipation.

"Congratulations, everybody," John says over the walkie. "Let's cause some chaos."

Cheers erupt over the farm and fill the twilight, sending an exodus of birds from the crops. David backs away from the gate and smiles at the sign that has thrilled and terrified him since he was a boy.

One Fright Only

CHAPTER 2

THE ONE-STORY HOUSE STANDS plainly among the neighbors' Halloween decorations. David wants to put out something to celebrate but does not want to perform the exhausting work of dragging the decorations from the basement. He could hang ghosts in the windows, but what was the point? Even if he wants to decorate for Halloween, he will only do so if he can dress it to the nines like his father had done every year, but that would be too much to tackle by himself. His brother is too little to be much help, and his mother...

Ada Earhart bursts out of the front door before he turns off the engine.

"You're late," she says loud enough for him to hear through the car's window.

"I'm sorry," he says as he grabs his laptop bag from the passenger seat and opens the door. He wants to tell her about staying behind to turn on the sign but realizes that's something a child would report after a fun day at school, not after work. She slides past him as he stands and sits in his place in the driver's seat, slinging her purse off her shoulder and placing it on the passenger seat. David steps away from the door, giving her space to close it.

"Wait," his mother motions him forward. "How was your day?"

"I'll tell you later," he laughs. "Get to work."

"Dinner's in the fridge," she says, turning on the car. His smile fades.

"I told you I'd make dinner."

"I had time." She waves a hand in the air to play it off. She either doesn't trust him to be responsible or doesn't believe he can cook. He's never had to, so he considers both might be true.

"Play with your brother and put him to bed."

David rolls his eyes, an affectation he's trying to shed. Taking care of his brother—spending time with him, making sure he is fed—is no longer a chore he can choose to be annoyed by.

"Love you," he says as his mother closes the door. She pulls out of the driveway too quickly to notice if a car is passing. He watches her turn the corner as though his attention will keep her safe. He turns back toward the house and notices the corner of the curtain closing in the bay window. David sighs and then enters the house.

Ethan fumbles with a PlayStation controller, struggling to pull his military character away from a group of opposing soldiers. Stopping to look out of the window gave his enemies enough time to surround him and end his round. A barrage of profanity erupts from the television speakers. David is about to remind Ethan that he is not allowed to play that game, until one of the voices addresses his little brother by the character's avatar's name, TJarvis32. Ethan is playing with the character their father created.

"Mom made Mac and cheese," Ethan throws over his shoulder.

"A 'please' might be nice," David says, which Ethan ignores. He heats a bowl of Mac and sets it on the floor by Ethan as he continues to play. He's too tired to tell his little brother to eat at the table. He walks into his bedroom and collapses into his desk chair; sitting in the dark, he stares at the pictures on the walls. Charcoal, acrylic, and pencil sketches of monsters and haunted houses are pinned up; some are his father's, but mostly his, and varying in quality, showing how much his skill has improved since he first picked up a crayon.

Among them are posters of his favorite horror movies, including *Scream*, *A Nightmare on Elm Street*, *House*, and *Friday the 13th: The Final Chapter*. His legs tingle from standing most of the day, and his hands are dry from the dirt in the farm air. A headache stems from the crick in the back of his neck.

I didn't even do anything strenuous. Is this stress? Is this how all adults feel?

The pixelated ghost that is the desktop's screensaver roams back and forth across the monitor, leaving an image of itself every few seconds to fill the screen, even though he turned the computer off before he left that morning.

"I told you not to use my computer," he yells into the living room.

"I needed it for homework!" his brother screeches. "Mom said!"

David swallows back his anger and moves the mouse. The ghost and its duplicates blink off, and the monitor brightens as the desktop displays. An illustration of Sally from *A Nightmare Before Christmas*, which he had illustrated years before, winks at him suggestively; tattered clothing missing more pieces than depicted on film as she lies in a graveyard, moon-bathing under a bright orange jack-o'-lantern.

His eyes linger on her body before he sees the tab on the desktop bar showing that a browser has been left open. He uses the mouse to click on it, and the tab grows into a window filled with colorful blocks. The program uses blocks to stack and create objects in a three-dimensional space. The basic outline, bright red body, and black squares for wheels are an obvious recreation of their father's truck that they had to sell to pay legal fees.

His stomach clenches. He closes his eyes, breathes in slowly, and when his lungs are full, he lets the air out in equal measures. He moves the cursor off the X and hits the dash symbol to minimize the window. He places his face in his hands and repeats his breathing.

The doorbell rings.

"I'll get it!" his brother yells from the living room. He hears the controller drop, and his brother's little feet stomp across the floor.

"Don't." He knocks down his chair as he rushes out of the room. Their mother has repeatedly told Ethan the rules about answering the door. Ethan holds it open, wearing a beaming smile. He backs away as Tracy walks into the house.

"Since when do you knock?" David asks.

Her brow furrows, and she looks at the door as though she isn't entirely sure. She tries to speak but is interrupted by a voice from outside.

"This isn't getting any lighter," Dougie says from the porch. Tracy moves aside to let him into the house, carrying a case of Budweiser.

"Just thought we'd hang out?" she says as though she is asking permission.

"Okay," David says. She's never had to ask for permission.

"And take advantage of your mother not being home," Dougie clarifies.

"I'm home," Ethan seethes as he gives Dougie a death stare.

"That's right, you are," Dougie replies. "Good job."

Ethan's face turns red as he turns to look at David. "You said we could watch a scary movie tonight," he whines.

"We'll see, little buddy."

"That's what Dad always says." Ethan slams the front door. David doesn't know what to say because his brother is correct. That is how their father replied when he worked late hours.

"How about you and I play a few rounds of your game for a little bit?" Tracy offers Ethan. He beams with joy and nods excitedly.

"Go get it set up," she says, and then winks at David.

Dougie walks into his room and resets the desk chair to sit in. He pulls a beer from the box and cracks the top. "So..." he says, taking a sip and handing David a beer. "Kyra."

The name and the implication almost make him blush. He sits on the bed and grabs a beer from the box. "There's nothing to tell."

"Oh, come on. Tell me what's going on."

"Nothing, really," he says, pulling on the tab and taking a sip. He tries to get past the bitterness. His father was so excited to give him a taste of his beer on his sixteenth birthday that he had to pretend he liked it. "She helped me pull up a scarecrow."

"I don't know. She volunteered to help pretty fast, and I've heard rumors that she's been talking about you a lot..."

"I'm sure she just feels bad for me."

"Well, sympathy sex is still sex."

David laughs and hits Dougie in the head with a pillow.

"She's five years older than me, and I'm broke and living with my mother. Besides, after this year with Dad..." He lets the implication linger.

"Maybe she likes bad boys?" Dougie offers.

"I can see that, but then what happens when she realizes I'm not bad?"

"Maybe it's time to add a little edge?"

"How do I do that?"

"Stop worrying about other people's feelings."

"You mean, just go for it?"

"Why not? Life's too short not to go for what you want."

David leans over and whispers, "Does Tracy seem off to you?"

Dougie's smile turns down. "You might want to talk to her about it."

The atypical seriousness confirms David's suspicions. "It's because of Dad, isn't it?"

"I think it's more than that, but I don't know."

"What you weirdos whispering about?" Tracy asks as she enters the room. "You look like you're about to kiss."

"It was gonna be romantic as hell," Dougie says. He grabs a beer and hands it to her as she sits next to David on the bed.

"I thought you were reserving that for Pam?" Tracy goads.

"Pam?" David gasps. "You?"

Dougie shrugs.

"He wishes," Tracy says, popping her tab. "He got all bothered when he heard she went out with Ryan the other night."

Dougie loses his playfulness and turns his attention towards the computer. David has known him long enough to see that he is bothered. "I didn't know you liked her."

"I didn't know he liked girls," Tracy laughs.

"Not like I see you with anyone," Dougie snaps at her. She shows him her middle finger before taking another sip. His friends often playfully bicker, but he can feel a sort of tension between them, so he cuts through it by offering a distraction.

"Get up for a second," he tells Dougie. Dougie complies and sits on the floor instead of taking his place next to Tracy. David opens his bag, takes out a small USB port, and plugs it into his desktop. A few keystrokes later, the same program that pulls the feeds from the main receiver box is installed on his computer. A window appears, showing a view of cornstalks and the front wheel of a tractor.

"Is that the farm?" Tracy asks and pulls herself to the top of the bed to look closer.

"It's all of it," David says. He clicks on the up arrow, and the screen changes to a view of the outhouse, the first stop on the hayride.

"That's awesome," Dougie says. He stands and leans over David's shoulder to press the up arrow rapidly. Images of the grounds blink by, as well as the inside of each attraction. "How many-"

"Ten altogether," David answers. "All the ones we are streaming on opening night."

"You little spy," Tracy shakes her head. David looks at her and sees the curl of her lips.

"No, I'm desperate," he says. He turns back towards the screen and slaps Dougie's hand away. He clicks rapidly until he sees an image high above the main grounds. From this vantage point, he can see the main concessions, a few game kiosks, the corner of the main building on the top right, and the haunted house in the middle of the left side. "I need to make sure everything goes smoothly."

"Or you want to catch something naughty," Dougie says.

"Like what, humping crows?" David says.

"Everyone fucks on the grounds after hours," Tracy rolls her eyes and then takes a sip of beer.

"Really?" David asks.

Dougie scoffs. "They're all sleeping with each other."

"Dougie feels left out," Tracy laughs.

"Like, everyone, everyone?" He thinks about Kyra.

"Yes," Tracy says, her jovial expression turning serious and almost angry. "Especially Kyra."

"That's not what I meant," David lies, then tries to change the subject and not think about his crush. "I'm just making sure nothing goes wrong."

"Trying to impress the bosses?" Dougie chides.

"Well, yeah. Hopefully, they'll hire me next year."

"I'm sure Kyra will want you," Dougie teases and then returns to the floor. David notices Tracy turn her face towards the bed.

"You okay?" he asks.

"She's jealous," Dougie answers for her.

"I'm not jealous," she says. "I just don't want to see you get hurt."

"I don't have a thing for Kyra," David retorts with more anger than he meant to. "I just think she's nice." He downs the rest of his beer.

"David!" Ethan calls from the other room.

"He probably wants more dinner," he says as he rises from the chair. He is not surprised that he is already feeling the wavering effects of the alcohol, considering he had only drunk three beers and a glass of wine in his entire life, a fact that he would not share with his friends. His father had a beer every night with dinner, and he often wondered what it tasted like, but the first time he snuck one into his room, he thought the can's contents had gone bad.

Ethan was watching a movie on the couch, looking bored and barely acknowledging David when his brother handed him the bowl.

"I just ate," he scowls without taking his eyes off a cartoon duck, placing a witch's hat on his head, and jumping into a pool of green paint. "You said you were going to watch a scary movie with me."

"We can tomorrow." He turns away, and the room sways.

"I'll tell Mom you were drinking."

David stops and turns back. "No, you won't, or I won't watch anything with you, ever."

"Dad watches movies with you every night before Halloween."

"Yeah, Ethan, he *did*," David emphasizes the last word and feels bad for doing so. He blames the alcohol for making him cruel but knows that is just an excuse. He returns to his room, where Tracy and Dougie stare at each other with less-than-friendly expressions.

"You okay?" David asks. Neither of his friends acknowledges his presence. After a few more seconds, Dougie slaps his knees and stands up from David's desk chair.

"I guess I have to go," he smiles widely and lifts the box of beer from the floor. He walks toward the door and stops next to David to slap him on the shoulder.

"You okay, man?" David asks.

Dougie smiles wider, looks from him to Tracy and back, then slides past him and out of the front door.

"What was that about?"

"Don't worry about it," Tracy says.

"Is he mad at me?" he asks, sitting in his desk chair.

Tracy unleashes a long sigh and pulls her curly hair from behind her head before lying down. The movement arches her back and stretches her shirt against her chest, prompting David to avert his eyes. He never saw Tracy as an attraction, but his body can't deny that she is attractive.

"John told us Elise resigned. Dougie told me they had a... thing, so he says."

"Elise? I thought she's dating Gabe."

"Oh, yes, she is, so don't say anything."

"So, you don't believe Dougie?"

She stares at the ceiling silently and then says, "I told him I believed him, but not because I think he would lie about it, but because Elise doesn't have standards and has hooked up with everyone else." She snorts a laugh and covers her mouth.

"That's pretty harsh," he says, also laughing and knowing it's the alcohol tickling his funny bone. "Dougie can be weird, but he wouldn't lie to us."

"Shit," she says, still laughing but with concern in her eyes. She turns onto her side, her hair cascading off the pillow and hanging off the edge of the bed. David takes another sip to hide the redness in his face. "Do you think I pissed him off?"

David shrugs, "Maybe he actually likes her?"

"That could have been her M.O.—convince people she was into them to string them along?"

"Why do you think she left?"

"Rumor says she was fucking John, too."

David leans forward in his chair. "He's twice her age."

Tracy leans forward as well. "Why do you think Gabe is leaving?"

Their faces are so close to each other that he smells the alcohol on her breath, mixed with her perfume. He leans back, emphatically, to justify his retreat. "That's wild." David notices a look of dissatisfaction. "Is something wrong?"

Tracy shrugs and rubs her finger along the knitting of David's comforter. A moment of silence hangs between them until she says, "You never thanked me, you know."

David searches for her meaning and realizes his mistake. "Oh, you're right. Thank you, Tracy. Really. I'm sorry I never said it."

"It's okay," she says without taking her eyes from the bed. "I don't need you to thank me, not really. I was just kind of hoping that us working together would let us spend more time together, especially since neither of us knows where we are going to be next year."

"Still looking at RISD?"

"That's the plan," she says. Tracy had her heart set on the Rhode Island School of Design since researching colleges during her junior year. She was told by a recruiter that she could be accepted based on grades alone, but since she has no photography, illustration, or painting portfolios, she isn't eligible for a scholarship. "I think I put together enough to get some financial help."

"At least you'll still be back for summer and holidays," David shrugs. "I'm assuming I'll be in town for the foreseeable future."

"What about New York or LA?"

"I can't afford that, not after this year, and I don't have time to apply for a scholarship. Since the story got picked up nationally, I'm sure a recruiter will trash my application the second they see my name."

"Even if any of it is true, they can't blame you for what your father's done."

"Yeah, but they will. What's that term, fruit from a poisonous tree?"

She lifts her eyes to stare into his. "Don't talk about your father like that."

David peels his eyes from her glare and says, "I need to put Ethan to bed soon."

"I can wait here until he goes to bed."

"I should spend time with him," he laments and stands.

"I get it," she sighs, swinging her legs over the side of the bed and standing. The narrow space between the bed and the chair forces their bodies together. Her eyes emit a melancholy he rarely sees from her. His father's actions have caused more than just uncertainty for his future, but also have caused him to question his friendships, because he can't help but think that Tracy's certainty in his father's innocence is an overcompensation for her true feelings; that his father did something horrible, and that he will end up exactly like him.

David hesitates toward the door. "I need to put him to bed, but—"

"No, I understand." She forces a smile and touches his arm. "He needs you."

"David, I'm tired," Ethan yells. He looks out of the doorway and back at Tracy. She leans around him and grabs the empty cans off the desk.

"I'll clean up," he says.

"It's fine. I got it." She waves her empty hand away without turning around.

David shuffles out of the room and into his brother's. Ethan is already in his pajamas and crawling into bed.

"You didn't need my help at all," he says.

"I need you to read to me," he says, but David is not paying attention. He walks over to the bookshelf and grabs a random book to throw onto his brother's bed.

"You can read that one. Go to sleep when you're done."

"You have to read to me," Ethan demands, a hint of sobbing in his voice that turns David's attention to see Ethan's bottom lip curl.

"I worked all day, Ethan."

"That's what Dad always says."

"Said. And now I understand why. I'm tired, and I have other things to do."

"But I can't sleep without a story," Ethan whines.

"Mom has to work, and I have to work, so you're going to have to grow up and do some things on your own. Read your book and go to bed."

Ethan pulls his Paw Patrol covers over his head. The bedding shakes as he sobs. David walks toward the bed and reaches out to comfort his brother but pulls his hand back. He regrets what he said but is unsure if it isn't the truth. He walks back into his room. Tracy is gone.

He sits at his desk and lifts the open can to his mouth, but the smell hits his nostrils first and causes his stomach to clench. He places the can back down and stares at the open view of the farm on his computer. He clicks the up arrow and sees the interior of the barn. Another click brings up the view of the dead-end circle in the middle of the corn maze, where one of the staff will be waiting with a horned, red devil mask and a fake scythe.

He clicks again, and a black eye stares back at him. David gasps and jumps against the back of his seat. The black orb pulls away to reveal a pointed beak that starts pecking at the lens. He scrolls through the rest of the cameras, which show the inside of the house attraction.

His father talked about seeing behind the scenes "at one of these things" every season they attended. Every time he thinks about being there, he feels guilty that his father isn't there with him, or that he should be working at a higher-paying job instead of one that he only took for nostalgia. He suspects his mother feels that way, but if she is bothered by it, she hasn't said so.

He clicks on the up arrow to the second-floor hallway where Dougie is stationed, and where he had seen Elise's shoe. Perhaps, he muses, Elise was murdered, and someone is cleaning up the evidence? He smiles and closes the computer.

His mind drifts to Kyra and considers the possibility of her liking him more than just another notch on her bedpost. He also considers whether being a notch on her bedpost is the worst that can happen. It doesn't matter, because no matter what Kyra is interested in, doing anything for himself will be selfish.

Life's too short not to go for what you want, Dougie said.

David shakes his head.

You're going to have to grow up, he told his little brother and immediately regretted it.

"You're going to have to grow up," he tells himself. He picks up the beer and chugs the bitterness down while listening to his brother's muffled cries.

Chapter 3

Tuesday, October 28th

For the first nineteen years of David's life, at least as far back as he can remember, Halloween season officially started when his father considered the weather cold enough to stop for a pumpkin-spiced coffee on his way to work. Starting in his pre-teen years, his father would take him to get an apple cider before dropping him off at school, and then send him in to do the ordering alone when he was old enough to handle the task.

David has been reluctant to continue the tradition in his father's absence, especially since he is not ready to relive such happy memories that have already been buried in the past, but caffeine addiction is stronger than nostalgia this morning, and he did not sleep well enough last night to function without coffee.

The sights and smells inside the Starbucks fill him with those childhood emotions. Paintings of grinning ghosts float across the surrounding windows. A jack-o'-lantern with a crooked smile is sketched on the chalkboard standing next to the check-out counter. The smell of coffee and cinnamon permeates the air.

A ska version of "Science-Fiction Double Feature" from *Rocky Horror Picture Show* plays through the speakers. Despite his father's absence, or maybe in spite of his father's absence, he lets his mind savor the nostalgia. The happiness is short-lived, as two cups are placed in front of him on the counter, one bearing his name and the other his father's, written in elaborate cursive.

Last year, David knew the fall ritual would be the last, but he thought it would be because he graduated and went off to college, not because of the horrors that led him to this morning.

"Haven't seen you guys this year," the barista smiles.

David stares at the Grande and Venti cups sitting on the counter.

"Everything okay?" Erin asks with a friendly smile. He remembers her name without having to look at her tag.

"I didn't pay for two," he mourns.

"It's cool," the young woman shrugs. "It's on the house."

"He'll appreciate it," he says, forcing a smile. He does not have the heart to correct her kindness. His loss does not have to bring her sadness. "Have a good day."

The young woman smiles warmly. "Tell your dad I said, 'Hi.'"

THE IRIDESCENT GREEN "ONE Fright Only" sign will stay lit until the morning after Halloween. The faces and frames of Halloween—skeletons, ghouls, bats, and other typical characters—hang from the fences on either side of the archway that leads into the park, heralding a night of thrills and chills. Even the ticket booth beyond the gate has had its facade decorated with fake siding to resemble the dilapidated wood of a rotting cabin.

The vendor stands and food trucks, along with the covered seating areas, have been populated with chairs, fresh coats of paint, and updated menus and title signs. The two large bonfires have been reinforced with new stone and towers of fresh wood. Mannequins stand silent and decorated across the grounds: a bloody clown, a monster made of tree vines, a pumpkin-headed chainsaw-wielding maniac.

Volunteers from the high school and community organizations will fill the space wearing costumes and walking the grounds to scare and help the patrons. They will arrive tonight for the dress rehearsal along with the food and game vendors, so David has been told. He had always wanted to be one of the scarers and hoped that being offered a job with the senior staff would afford that position, but they picked him for his video experience. Just as good, he thinks, as he gets to watch every single person going through every single haunt get scared out of their gourds.

The low rumble of a tractor's engine and its squeaking gate quicken David's pace around the fairgrounds. Coffee splashes from the tiny lips of his to-go cups and burns the back of his hand, but the excitement overcomes the pain. He had been awakened by a text from Tracy inviting him to ride the main attraction with the other seniors on their first run. He thought he would have to vicariously witness the fun while watching others enjoying the rides from behind the scenes, but being able to go on the hayride grants an opportunity to continue a decade-old tradition. Excited still, even though he knows that without his father, the tradition is already dead.

Tracy is standing behind the tractor and watching the rest of the senior staff climb the steps into its trailer. He misses his father, but Tracy has accompanied them at least two Halloweens over the years, so at least part of the tradition is being carried on in spirit.

Then, he considers who else is joining the ride. Mark and Ryan are throwing him glares and laughing. They might not be talking about him, but he knows they won't let him enjoy the ride without ridiculing him at least once. Pam is pulling from a vape in the corner and talking to Gabe, sitting on the opposite side, next to Dougie, Kyra, and Mark's twin, Kevin. He can tell the twins apart because Mark has a soul patch, but otherwise, they are identical. Some are other college-age students who are villains in the house and maze, and the older riders are most likely some of the engineers and builders John hires to keep the effects running.

"Tracy," David says as he approaches. She turns and smiles, eyeing the cups in his hands.

"David!" Kyra stands and waves from the trailer. "Saved you a seat!"

His face flushes, and Tracy notices. She sees her jaw steel as she looks from Kyra to David.

"She's just looking out for me, being new."

"I'm glad she is looking out for you," Tracy says, but her face betrays her words.

"We can sit together." He offers her a cup of coffee.

"It's crowded," she says, and walks toward the game tent in the main area.

"Tracy," David calls after her.

"Oh, shit," Ryan says. "Trouble in paradise?"

David ignores him and walks up the steps. Kyra looks up at him from the hay-riddled bed with a furrowed brow. "What's he yapping about?"

"No one ever knows," Dougie says, saving David from answering. Ryan turns red and opens his mouth at Dougie, but then closes it. Everyone except Dougie is confused by Ryan's retreat, who continues to stare at him until he is forced to look away. David makes a mental note to ask Dougie what that's about. His attention turns back to the field as he watches Tracy walk out of view behind one of the concession stands.

"Let it go," Dougie whispers as he shuffles across the hay to make room to sit between him and Kyra. He knows Dougie doesn't like sweet coffee, so he offers it to Kyra. "Do you like pumpkin spice?"

"Love it," she overemphasizes, "thank you."

David leans towards Dougie and whispers, "I don't know what I did."

"It's about what you will do," he says, and nods towards Kyra.

"Who the hell is Luke?" Mark laughs as he reads the name on the cup. David turns towards Mark and leans forward to speak, but Kyra interjects. Her eyes tell him to stay calm as she sips, so he leans back against the wood. She scoots closer to him. Mark rolls his eyes and looks away. Ryan, however, has never paid much attention. David wonders if he should feel bad that Ryan's jealousy fills him with satisfaction.

A large-framed man in denim overalls lifts the stairs and locks them to the back of the trailer.

"Thanks, Mitchell," Kyra says, to which the older man grunts. He rounds the trailer and sits in the driver's seat.

"He's been working as the field manager for the farm since before Lillian was born," Kyra whispers to David. "There had been a rumor that he was going to inherit it when Lillian's parents passed because she was still in college, but it all went to her."

"He must not be too resentful, if he still works for her."

Kyra lifts an eyebrow and smiles. "Or he's waiting for the right opportunity."

"Wow, you're dark," David laughs.

Kyra flexes both eyebrows. "You have no idea, Shaggy."

The tractor lurches forward and rides the dirt path around the cornfield. The silence of the fairground diminishes gradually as the trail bends and the tractor takes them away from the rest of the attractions. Only the tops of the rides in the main area can be seen beyond the stalks.

A lone outhouse comes into view on the side of the road, recessed into the crop. David hopes that Kyra doesn't notice how much his body tenses with anticipation. The outhouse is the only part of the ride that hasn't changed since he was nine years old. The tractor halts, sending his body forward to collide with Kyra. He sips his coffee to hide the red that flushes his cheeks.

A bang on the door erupts from the inside of the closed outhouse. Mark looks around the trailer. This is his scare, so he doesn't know who is in there. Everyone turns their head to look towards the stalks. The banging on the outhouse is a misdirection. David had never forgotten his first time on the ride.

They lurched to a halt. The bang on the door. He had already been on edge, waiting for something to pop out, when the hockey mask-wearing, chainsaw-wielding madman ran out of the stalks and jumped on the side of the trailer. The chainsaw revved above him.

He pissed his pants.

His father told him, "Next time, you'll know exactly where the scary is coming from, so you'll have the upper hand." The year after, his father held him close, even though he was not afraid. Well, not as scared as the year before.

"I looked on the other side 'cause that's where the scare was coming from," David proudly told his father. His father approved.

"Intelligence beats chainsaw every time."

Now, they wait to see the stalks move or hear rustling. Instead, the outhouse door bursts open. David jumps. Kyra grabs onto him and laughs. The others in the trailer start cheering at the pumpkin-faced killer wielding a chainsaw and laughing maniacally.

"Misdirection is omnidirectional," his father told him while they were watching *Invasion of the Body Snatchers* when David was ten. The pumpkin kills the chainsaw and lifts his mask off to reveal his face.

"Welcome to Hell, ladies and gentlemen," John says, opening his arms.

Everyone claps.

"I couldn't resist," he shrugs. "Mitchell will stop for a few minutes at each set so Kyra can fill you in on some of this year's additions. Keep your eyes open for something we can add to the show. Let's make it memorable."

John lifts his mask back over his head and pulls the chainsaw starter. It revs back to life, and the workers in the trailer erupt with cheers. He jumps down and walks into the cornfield. The trailer lurches again, and again, David's body bumps Kyra.

"Don't enjoy that too much," she laughs as she notices the smile spreading across his face.

But it wasn't the casual touch that made his heart race. He had been jump-scared and is still feeling the effects. There are so many emotions that he thought he might never feel as he grew older and more mature. Having lived through true fear and loss, he never thought he would, or should, be scared by entertainment. Yet, his skin feels goosebumps that have nothing to do with the cold. And he loves it.

The trailer continues into the forest that encompasses the field. The canopy blocks the sun and darkens the view enough for David to believe nighttime is here and Halloween has come to shroud the living realm. Up ahead, Dorothy and the Seven Dwarves await to greet the tractor, the cardboard stands beaten up and stained with mud and old bird droppings.

On the opposite side of the trail is a troupe of taxidermic white owls sitting on a tree branch that arches over the tractor. Most of them have big white eyes with bright blue irises, save for the owl in the middle that only has one. Their fake fur is also stained with mud, with a few chunks missing, revealing metal wiring.

"I always wondered, when did they stop updating the kids' stuff?" he asks Kyra.

"Since, like the nineties, bro," Kevin answers.

"Lillian's father didn't want to charge families for the daytime rides," Kyra explains, "but they couldn't afford to pay staff to keep it running. When Lillian took over, she left it to rot." She shrugs and looks disappointed.

The tractor bears right and passes a cardboard facade of a castle with a princess painted in a window surrounded by wooden, painted cartoon critters in various forms of decay, looking up at her from the forest floor. "My dad used to tell me these were left by children who were eaten by the monster that took over the ride."

"How old were you when he told you that?" asks Kyra.

"Yeah," David smiles, "I'm starting to see how that can be problematic." She laughs with him, but then tilts her head in curiosity.

"Tell me about him."

He peruses the faces around the trailer, his memories morphing them into those from across a decade. Teenagers wearing grunge flannel when he was a preteen, a couple wearing matching "Just Married" shirts when he was in middle school, and a girl named Jillian Podzanski, whom he had a crush on that same year, gave him his first kiss inside the haunted maze. He could see every one of them clearly, as though every memory was created the day before.

"Maybe another time," he smiles politely as he says it. Her nod, along with her large, expressive eyes, shows him that she understands.

After plodding through a copse of trees filled with zombified critters, the trailer stumbles upon the face of a cabin illuminated from the ground by two spotlights at each end. The facade has been painstakingly constructed and painted to resemble the face of a real cabin. The wear and tear on the wood and glass over the years help make it look more realistic.

Each year, the theme of the cabin changes. When he was eleven, it was an old woman who sat in a rocking chair, and when the trailer stopped, she screamed for her hillbilly sons to "Round 'em up for supper!"

They burst out of the front door, hooting and hollering, and then attacked the trailer. When he was seventeen, someone dressed as a bear pulled a corpse from the house and then growled in the air. More bears charged the trailer from the woods on the other side. The trailer stops. Kyra leans into him and whispers in his ear. Her lips touch his earlobe, and it sends a quake through his body.

"Wait for it."

The silhouette of a spider crawls from the cabin's right side. Its shape and thickness mimic a tarantula, and its movement is identical. One of the older men unleashes a playful sound of disgust that causes the others to laugh. The spider crawls towards the right window, pivots downward, and then moves around it to reach the front door. It moves down the door and disappears as it reaches the bottom, giving the illusion that it has crawled underneath.

Another spider crawls from under the roof's awning at the top left and towards the door, followed by another from the top and three more from the right. Each is a different shape and size. As dozens of tarantula shadows overtake the front of the house, a guitar riff screams from the amplifiers around the trailer.

David recognizes the song from the first chord. "In-A-Gad-da-Da-Vida," by Iron Butterfly. The song was used in the fifth sequel to *A Nightmare on Elm Street* in one of his father's favorite scenes. An unlucky teen victim gets high, passes out, and in the 'Dream World' gets sucked into a television before being tortured inside a video game. His father would laugh every time, even though the idea of being stuck in a video game scared David when he was younger. It was cool that the character gained powers, but the evil characters were more powerful, and he was trapped in a place that had no rules and no way out.

The house's facade becomes overrun with crawlers as the song's deep, guttural vocals begin. The shadows then retract as they squeeze under the doorframe at the bottom until the cabin face once again stands plain, every spider now inside. Another five seconds pass until the door bursts open.

Two hairy black fangs squeeze through the door and reach out towards the trailer. The onlookers on that side back away as the pointy fangs stop inches away. Two legs reach from around either side of the cabin, creating the illusion that the spider is bursting out of it. A semicircle of eight red eyes rises above the roof. Half of the participants gasp while a few others laugh.

Although the trees are blocking the sun, the environment is illuminated enough that David can see the row of LED lights creating the eyes and the two puppeteers holding the backs of the arms on either side. The illusion will look flawless at night. Hell, it's still effective even given the visible seams during the day.

"Damn," he says loud enough for Kyra to hear. "Your idea?"

"I also wanted someone to throw plastic spiders into the trailer while it was happening, but Lilly said it would be too scary." She winks.

"I bet John loved it, though."

"I learned from the best," she shrugs. She's looking around at the other patrons, elated over their reactions, and then yells loud enough to overtake the music. "Kevin will be stationed here to make sure the physical performers are in place and start the show."

"Yay," Kevin moans.

"Not the role you wanted?" Dougie asks.

"I like being a scarer."

"He loves terrifying children," his twin says.

"That's why he's afraid of me," Kevin replies.

"He's the evil twin," Mark laughs.

The trailer jerks forward as the music starts to lower and the set pieces retract behind the house. Mannequins and animatronics of a werewolf and zombie limbs moving beneath tombstones fill the sides of the trail, their effects softened by a lack of dramatic lighting. The trailer turns left and then right until it faces a barn with open doors flanking the trail on either side. Having gone through the barn every year for over a decade, David notices it has been recently painted and reinforced with fresh wood at its edges.

"We gave it some plastic surgery," Kyra whispers, reading his mind. "We have to dress to impress this year."

"Why's that?"

"I'll tell you later," she nods towards the others, engaged in their hushed conversations, but still within listening distance.

The tractor leads the trailer through the opening and towards the exit on the other side. The exit doors slowly shut, forcing the tractor to stop in the middle of the barn. Then, the barn doors they had entered through shut, trapping them inside. Shafts of light cut through the darkness from man-made holes in the roof, too round and pointedly placed to be caused by random wear and tear.

"Spotlights," she tells him.

"How do you keep reading my mind?" he asks.

"You're a video guy," she shrugs. "You look for the cause behind the effect." She toasts him with her coffee cup, then stands and walks toward the front of the trailer, hay crunching under her feet. She turns to address the riders.

"In the past, there was a bunch of recycled hillbilly nonsense happening—"

"Yeah, there was!" Ryan yells. Kevin cups his hands around his mouth to unleash a howl.

"As you can tell, two of those inbred assholes are on this ride." Everyone laughs. Ryan and Kevin give a thumbs up and two big smiles.

"This year, we have a fire element in play." She pulls a laser pointer out of her jacket pocket and traces a black line that runs the length of the room on the side of the vehicle. The hay has been pulled back from the area, and red tape outlines the hose that has been laid into the ground.

"The fire will plume up in several areas and then build up to unleash a full wall as the grand finale. We're not going to run it right now since we need to run it for the fire inspector first."

"Boo!" Pam protests.

"I know, but if all goes well, we can do the whole thing during dress rehearsal Thursday night. My station on show night will be outside at the control panel so I can close the doors, start the effect, and reopen the doors. In case there is a power outage, the mechanism to open the doors has a failsafe that can open the door by a battery-powered remote, which Mitchell will have with him."

Mitchell lifts the remote.

"Good job, Boss," Ryan mocks while slow-clapping.

"Remember, if there is an accident, it's okay to leave Ryan to die."

Everyone except Ryan laughs and cheers. Kyra takes a bow and then walks back to sit next to David.

"He can dish it out but not take it, I guess," David whispers to her as he gazes at Ryan's red, angry face.

"That's one of the reasons he's my ex," she says, a little louder than her previous whispers.

Ryan turns away to look at the empty room. Light floods the space as the doors on the other side of the barn open and the ride moves along. David's phone vibrates in his pocket. His stomach clenches, thinking he might have just received a text from Tracy. He owes it to her to answer, so he pulls his phone from his inside pocket and reads the preview message. He doesn't recognize the number.

It's Gabe. Check for... He opens the phone. *It's Gabe. Check for camera placement in the lab. I was leaving it until the last minute for the electrical work to be set.*

"Everything okay?" Kyra asks.

"Yeah, Gabe wants me to check the camera placement in the lab," he texts as he talks. *No problem.*

"Oh, yeah, he was afraid the electrical ladders would fry them up or interfere."

Kyra will show you the effects. Find a place high up. We can pad it with rubber.

Will do, David responds.

The tractor stutters as it takes a slight incline. When the trail straightens, a structure similar to the barn lies ahead, but the outside has been painted silver and fitted with brass bars and fake wiring to resemble something akin to a giant battery.

"That's a hell of a decorating job," David tells Kyra. He must not have spoken quietly enough because Kevin answers, "Thanks."

"Yes, Kevin," Kyra mocks him like a child, "It's your baby."

"Still, John's idea," Mark says.

"Fuck off," Kevin snaps at his brother. Ryan laughs.

"Boys," Kyra rolls her eyes.

The sound of electricity ushers the trailer through the opening as though it is traveling into another realm. A bolt of lightning sparks to their left, eliciting gasps of surprise. It arcs from one side of the stage area to the other, connected by two large cylinders to create an electric arc that illuminates that side of the room. Between them are two metal tables, each covered in a white cloth and spotlighted by two lamps hanging directly above them from a loft. Two smaller cylinders are placed on either side of the entrance and exit, creating the illusion that the lighting is trapping them inside.

"This is awesome," David says, feeling that little-boy glee once again rising from inside and breaking his adult mask.

"John's idea, but Gabe knew how to make it work," Kyra explains. "Well, knew how to make it work safely." The tables under the lightning arc tip forward to slam their edges onto the ground. "This is where Pam and Ryan will rush the trailer," she yells over the real and artificial sounds pumping through speakers on the other side of the room.

David fishes his phone out to text Gabe: *This is awesome. Well done.*

Three dots appear on the screen, followed by the reply: *Doesn't matter if no one sees it. Have Kyra turn off the effects and see if you can find a place to hang a camera.*

David shows Kyra the text. She hops over the right side of the vehicle to unlock a utility box on the wall with a key. She thumbs a few buttons on the breaker. The electricity dissolves, and the music dies. Another switch turns on two large lights hanging from the ceiling, which illuminate the entire room.

"Stretch your legs, people," she commands.

Mitchell hops off the tractor and opens the trailer's gate. David stands and looks around the room as everyone else exits. He immediately understands why Gabe wanted to wait until the last minute.

Glare from the electricity is going to be a problem, he texts to Gabe.

Yes, comes the simple response.

He walks down the steps and heads beyond the tilted operating tables until he sees a wooden ladder on the back wall, hanging from a door in the ceiling. The softness of the wood reveals its age, so he takes every rung carefully. The loft is mostly barren, save for an apple cart with items sitting on it at the far end. He walks until he is leaning over the side and looking directly down at the trailer. He looks back towards the wall and sees a closed window.

We can clamp a camera onto the edge of the loft. If we use one of the mini sports cams with a wide lens, you'll be able to see the tables and the side of the trailer. Might look the right amount of funky.

Done, Gabe replies.

David takes a breath and feels a sense of accomplishment wash through his body. It wasn't a hard test, but as long as he appears to pull his weight on this job, he can be proud of his work. He turns to leave when a glint of light from the pile of objects against the wall catches his eye. He walks over to the pile and notices that it's the brown robe that will be worn by the senior staff that year.

David kneels and pulls on it, revealing its accompanying pumpkin masks underneath. Next to the mask is a cell phone, whose face is glowing pale blue as it receives an app update reminder. Behind the reminder is the wallpaper for the screen, and he recognizes that the woman in the center of the crowd is Elise.

Beside the phone and mask is a small trowel used for gardening. It's caked in rust, and a darker, redder substance stains the bladed edge. He touches that part with his finger and scrapes, flaking the redness off without much pressure, telling him it is not rust but possibly—

Stop, he tells himself. *Don't go down that rabbit hole.*

An image of his father plays in his mind's eye, or rather, the video footage that continues to play in his head like a waking nightmare.

Stop!

Wood creaks behind him, and he turns around in time to see Ryan reaching for his chest and grabbing his shirt in both fists. He pulls David to the side so that he is leaning over the edge of the loft.

"Stay the hell away from Kyra," Ryan seethes, his face beet red, jaw clenched. Panic sets in as his body teeters over the trailer, a good twenty-foot drop onto metal tables.

"I'm just trying to help," David says as he grabs Ryan's wrist. If Ryan wants to drop him, there is nothing David can do to prevent it.

"That's how she traps you. She makes you feel useful. You're not useful." He moves his arm a few inches forward, forcing David to cling to the edge with the tips of his shoes.

"Okay, I'm not useful," David says, his eyes shifting between the angry man and the metal below. Ryan's arm begins to shake, and his face somehow grows a darker shade of red. A vein forms on his temple. David realizes that Ryan is not just trying to be intimidating or reacting out of jealousy; he is genuinely enraged.

"Seriously, I'm not..."

Ryan pushes him further out.

"Ryan, enough!" Mark calls out from the back of the loft. Ryan's face lightens a shade, but he continues to stare daggers into David's eyes as Mark approaches. "Seriously, man. He doesn't know anything."

Ryan takes his eyes away from David to look at Mark, seemingly confused by his words.

"Don't let her get in the way," Mark says. Ryan pulls David back enough for him to stand on the loft. David tries to move around Ryan, but the other man points a finger at his chest.

"Do not get involved," he warns.

"Got it," David says, holding up his hands and backing towards the ladder. He takes it down quickly and walks towards the trailer. Kyra stops him in the center of the room.

"You look like you've seen a ghost," she says. "You okay?"

David takes a deep breath and releases it. "Yeah, a lot of dust up there."

"Oh," she says, noticing Mark and Ryan coming down the ladder. Her expression changes from worried to angry. "Oh," she moves toward the ladder.

"It's okay," David says as he steps in front of her, eyes pleading for her to let it go. "I just want to do my job."

"Sorry for their immaturity."

"It's fine," David lies. "But someone has unresolved issues." He nods towards Ryan, jumping down off the fifth rung.

"More than you know," Kyra says. "They won't bother you anymore."

"Please don't say anything," David pleads.

"I won't. There are other ways I can make sure they behave."

"How do you mean?"

"A lot is going on with the senior staff that it's better you not know about. I mean that in a legal sense. Some of us have been here far too long."

"How dangerous is he?" David asks.

"All bark, no bite. No bite, whatsoever." Kyra grabs David's arm and escorts him back to the trailer. He can feel Ryan's eyes burning a hole in his head.

As the ride ends, patrons can choose to take the maze back into the main fairgrounds or head south towards the haunted house. Since most of the workers need to return to work, the group takes the trail around the field and spreads away to their various duties. Kyra stops before the stone trail that leads up the hill to the Badger's house.

"I need to check in with John and Lilly," she nods towards the house.

"I should get back to Gabe," David says.

"Thanks for the hard work," she says, offering him a pleasant smile before walking up the hill.

She is perfect in every way.

He is immediately embarrassed by the cliché.

She is not really into someone four years younger anyway. She's just being kind because she knows what you've been through. She saw the footage. She saw the horror. She invited you out of pity.

Pity for the boy whose father is a murderer.

CHAPTER 4

LILLIAN WALKS INTO THE kitchen area from the back room where the equipment is housed. "Oh," she stops at the entranceway, "David."

"Didn't mean to scare you. Sorry."

"No problem," she says, although she still looks frazzled at his presence. "I thought you were doing the hayride?"

"It's over," David says. "I can come back later if...?"

"No, it's fine," she puts up her hands and waves towards the back room. "It's David," she calls into the room, which David can only guess is Gabe she's talking to. "How was the ride?"

She leans against the doorframe and folds her arms to look like she is having a casual conversation, but the way she does it dictates an uncomfortableness that he can't identify. David realizes he has either interrupted a private conversation or Lillian doesn't want to be alone in a room with someone she hardly knows...or knows about his past.

"Great, as always. Lots of cool new stuff." He tries not to smile too hard. She looks back in the room and then back at David. "I was just going over the finer details with Gabe. We have a lot riding on this little streaming stunt of John's."

"You don't think it will work?" David asks.

"I can only hope. If we don't at least double our intake from last year, there won't be a next year." She sits at the kitchen table and leans on her arms as she stares out of the shack. Her face changes to one more resembling her age. "Now, with John leaving, I don't know if we can pull it off next year, anyway."

"John is leaving?" The surprise bursts out of him. This must have been the information Kyra referred to.

"This is his last year. I guess we aren't lucrative enough for him anymore."

"I heard that the farm was in trouble," David offers, trying not to add too much speculation.

"You heard correctly. The state has steadily raised property taxes for years while importing out-of-state crops. This..." she waves her hand in the air, "amusement... is our biggest money grab for the year. We're on life support."

"Is that why you made the attraction one night only instead of every weekend in October?"

"Disappointing, I know. We tried to get out a loan, but since I had to take so many out for the farm over the years..."

David didn't know how loans worked, but if a farm that has been lucrative for most of its lifespan is unable to borrow money to stay afloat, he understands the implication.

"Not your fault. Work hard, have fun, get a paycheck." Her tone is mocking, leaving David not knowing how to respond. The words echo advice his father had given him when he volunteered at an ice cream parlor the summer before senior year.

"I'll let you guys get to it." She walks towards him, stops, and then awkwardly pats him on the shoulder. "Make us look amazing," she says before she leaves.

Gabe is sitting in the torn leather chair in front of the monitors, clicking on the control panel and scrolling through the eight camera feeds in the haunted house.

"I'm sorry if I interrupted something," David says.

"Nothing to interrupt," he answers while still clicking through feeds. "I asked if I could have my last payment as a check before leaving tomorrow instead of a direct deposit."

"Oh," David says, even though Lillian told him a different conversation had taken place. "Did it go well?"

Gabe swivels the chair around. "Lilly never wants to give up money, but considering I've been doing this since I was seventeen, she had to comply." His dry, emotionless expression does not give away his happiness about the result.

"Great," he says, trying to think of anything else to say. Gabe nods his head then swivels back to face the monitors.

"The mini and clip stands are on the shelves. Go set that up, and I'll connect the feeds here."

"Great," David says again, walking to the shelves lining the back of the room. He searches through the piles of wires, USB converters, and other audio/visual equipment. Gabe had shown him where everything is stored during orientation the month before, but he can't remember which shelves the stands are on.

"Someone left a phone in the loft. I think it might be Elise's since her picture is the wallpaper." A few seconds pass without a sound, and when David turns around, he sees Gabe staring at him.

"Never mind, I'll do it," Gabe says and then walks towards him. "You stay here and install the receiver into the converter." Gabe kneels and grabs a small camera and a stand with screwable clips, and two black boxes. "I recommend checking all the cameras before opening." He hands David one of the black boxes, a signal receiver, then grabs a walkie from one of the battery stands on the shelf. He leaves the room.

David wonders if he has done or said something to upset Gabe. Maybe he took too long to find the camera? The chair squeaks as David collapses into it. If he has irritated Gabe, he will just add that to the list of people he has pissed off without meaning to, because he can't shake the exchange with Tracy. He pulls his phone out of his jeans and texts her: *I'm sorry about this morning.*

He wonders how long it will take her to reply, and what that length of time would mean, but his phone vibrates before he can place it on the desk.

No, I'm sorry. I just get crazy when it comes to Kyra.

Why? He replies, and wonders if that is how he would normally reply had he not been distracted by his budding attraction for Kyra.

Tracy replies quickly: *she goes through guys like a knife through butter.*

Was he her "guy?" If so, he doesn't think he cares if she wants to go through him like butter. For someone as attractive as Kyra, both in body and mind, he might be okay with being her next victim. He knows that's his hormones talking, and he needs to shake them away if he is going to focus on work and taking care of his family.

Besides, she's just being kind because of what happened to his father, the same tragedy that put him in this place. Because of that, his life is no longer his own. He has a family that needs his help. A family that needs him to grow up faster than they had planned. David sinks into the chair. If Kyra likes him, he should let her down now. End this before anything gets started. His reality has to come before his fantasies.

He sends another text: *I think she's just being nice.*

Dots on the screen appear, then disappear. Then, they reappear. After a minute of starting and stopping, she replies, *I don't want to see you hurt.*

"Ready for the receiver," Gabe says through the walkie on the desk.

David plugs the receiver into the input hub behind the monitor bay. Every camera signal is fed into that box and then output to the monitors. It has a built-in modem that can be accessed remotely, which is what his laptop is connected to. The website will stream using the flat screen's monitoring program instead of pulling the individual video signals from the box to save bandwidth. The program allows everyone watching to choose which feeds they want to see at any moment and switch between them at will.

He grabs the mouse and clicks on several buttons to have the program search for a new transmission source. The blank square is replaced by a close-up image of Gabe's nostrils.

"You have some bats in the cave," David says.

"Bats?" Gabe leans back, and his confused face fills the image.

"Something my dad used to say when I had boogers hanging out of my nose. I'm kidding."

"Oh," Gabe says, pinching his nostrils between his fingers.

"Is that her phone?" David asks.

"Oh... umm... There's nothing here." He leans back and turns the camera towards the wall where the phone and the costume had been piled.

"Oh, weird."

"Not really. It was probably one of the techies putting it there before the ride. They all hang out together. Setting the shot now."

He tries to remember the faces of the other women with Elise in the phone's wallpaper and if he had seen any of them around the grounds, but he hadn't been concentrating on them enough to remember.

"How's it look?" Gabe asks. The image rotates until it shows the two tables at the bottom and the length of the space from one side to where the tractor and trailer will be parked.

"Perfect."

"On my way back."

David muses over an uneasy feeling. The ominous sensation of leaving the house knowing that there is something he didn't take, or when an image looks strange but he can't identify what is out of place. He shakes his head. He considers that he might be worried about what will happen between him and Kyra, but his stomach is where that brand of nervousness lies. The uneasy feeling in his mind is something else. What had he noticed?

Chapter 5

Dr. Grant is standing in the middle of Brooke Drive and Rumor Lane, holding a stop sign and directing a line of children to cross the street. Ethan is sauntering behind the other children, hiding under his sweater's hood and looking down at the ground. David thinks about beeping the car horn to get Ethan's attention, but realizes he might scare the kids.

He'll also avoid grabbing the attention of the volunteer crossing guard, his dentist, whom he hasn't visited in almost a year. He hates the feeling of the metal tools scraping against his teeth. A childish thought, but at least he now has the excuse of wanting to save the copay for his brother to save the family some money.

Then again, it is Halloween. Sheriff Brackett's line from the movie Halloween comes to mind: "Everyone is entitled to one good scare."

He places his hand on the horn but thinks better about pushing it.

See, Mom, I'm maturing.

David drives home and waits on the porch for Ethan to arrive. When he does, his little brother races up the stairs and wraps his arms around his waist.

"Why were you walking home alone today?" he asks.

Ethan unlatches from his brother's waist, looks down at the porch, and shrugs his shoulders. David kneels so that he can pull Ethan's attention.

"What's wrong, E-man?"

"Don't call me that," Ethan snaps.

"I'm sorry," David says, not realizing he called Ethan anything besides his name. "I was just excited to see you."

Ethan ignores him and opens the door to rush inside. David follows and finds his mother sitting on the couch, flummoxed as her youngest son ignores her greeting and runs down the hall to slam his bedroom door.

"What was that about?" She asks.

"I have no idea. None of his friends were talking to him on the walk home."

His mother makes a curious noise. David sits on the loveseat that is turned towards the couch. "Don't you have to go?"

"I'm heading in late and working a little later."

"Why?"

She jerks her head to the side, her way of shrugging.

"What?"

"I wanted to see you guys for a few extra minutes." Her words are thick, as though she is about to cry. "How was your day?"

The question is obvious and routine, especially when he was in school, but he doesn't know how to respond now that he's an adult. Instead of answering with a noncommittal "fine" like he would when he got home from school, he considers the multiple experiences and decides to add more weight to his answer.

"These people are strange," he says.

"Let me guess, drama between coworkers, some are sleeping with each other, others are jealous that some are sleeping with each other, there is more than one boss, and the bosses don't like each other?"

"Holy shit, Mom."

"That's what every job is like when you're an adult," she scoffs. "Some children never grow up. Their bodies get older, but their minds are still juvenile."

"And you do this until you die?"

"Pretty much. Sorry. You'll learn to adapt when you go to college. It's a good buffer."

"Mom." His voice sours.

"Save it, David. I'm not in the mood."

"We can't afford it."

"You have excellent SAT scores and will get either a scholarship or a grant. Even if not, I'll get another job. You have to go to college."

"Most trades don't even need a degree anymore."

"You're not doing a trade. You're going to get a degree and do something that will save you money without sacrificing your time or health."

"That's exactly what Dad did—"

"The situation your father and I were in forced us to make choices without knowing what it meant for our lives. You get to learn from our mistakes."

"You mean me. I was the mistake."

"No, David." She looks at him with fire in her eyes. "You were what we chose because of our mistake, and never regretted it, but it did change our lives. Your father left college to support us. You have foresight because of that. Use it."

Looking into his mother's eyes, he realizes the fire inside of her is fueled by anger. An idea occurs that he had never considered before, and he instantly wants to deny it, but his mother's anger reveals more of the story than her words. "You didn't want to have me. He did."

"For fuck's sake, David." She stands and grabs her purse from the couch. "I have to go." She is halfway towards the front door when David stops her dead in her tracks.

"Were you in love with Dad when you had me?"

She stops and breathes in before speaking. David digs his fingernails into the armchair.

"I love your father with all of my heart, and the life we built, but you deserve to live the life you carve for yourself."

David wants to protest, but she hurries out of the door. He places his hands on his face and feels a sob climb up his throat. He is about to unleash it when he realizes his right jeans pocket is too heavy. He walks to the door and opens it in time to see his mother reaching out for the doorknob. He fishes the car keys out of his pocket and hands them to her. They stand silently for a few seconds, regarding each other's presence and tears.

"I didn't know if I wanted to spend the rest of my life with your father when I got pregnant with you, but we were in love. All I'm asking is that if you are going to follow in his footsteps, don't put your shoes exactly in his footprints. Be a good man like him, but be a little more pragmatic with the decisions that lead you to the future you choose."

"How will I know the right choice when I have to make it?"

"That's the hard part," she laughs. "But I'm here to help."

"Thanks, Mom." He leans in, and they embrace.

"My first way of helping you to make good choices is to help you not make the same mistakes we did, so I placed condoms in your top drawer."

"Mom!" He leans out of the hug and looks at her with surprise.

"Please be careful and be a gentleman." She turns around and hurries down the steps towards her car, leaving David in shock on the steps. "And with who? No one likes me."

"Sure," she says, as though she knows something he doesn't. "Just don't do it tonight. Spend time with your brother, or I will be furious." She shuts the car door and drives away. David watches her leave and then turns around to see Ethan standing in the room.

"What's condoms?" he asks.

David's mind panics for an answer and then lands on "Candy."

"Can I have some?"

Shit. "No, I mean, it's vitamins. For grown-ups."

"You're not a grown-up."

"I'm nineteen. You're a grown-up when you turn eighteen."

"That's just a number. That doesn't mean you're grown-up."

Ethan's adorable perceptiveness is turning annoying. "When you don't crap your pants by accident in the middle of the night, then you're an adult." His brother's face immediately twists into anger and hurt, and though he used to get a kick out of pushing his brother's buttons, the reaction leaves him disappointed.

"Why don't I make us some mac & cheese and watch a movie? Your pick."

The joy on his little brother's face fills him with the same. "Can we watch *Jack Skellington?*"

David's joy deflates. His little brother doesn't know that they canceled every streaming service to save money, so the only way to watch it is to go through Dad's movie collection in his office. He forces a smile back onto his face for Ethan's benefit and says, "Sounds perfect. Go play some games until I get dinner ready, and then we'll watch it together."

Ethan runs towards the television while David walks into the hallway and readies himself to open the door at the end of the hallway. He places his hand on the knob and closes his eyes.

Another life needs me right now, and that should take precedence over my anger.

He turns the knob and pushes the door. The setting sun bathes the room in a pink glow. He is not ready to acknowledge the items around the room, so he overcompensates by concentrating on the dust floating through the air. He hopes to rely on that tunnel vision to carry him toward the DVD shelf without looking around the room but is betrayed by his other senses.

The room smells like a mix of aftershave and paint. Not just abrasive but persuasive, insisting that a specific life is still alive and toiling away on its hobbies. He concentrates on reading the spines of the DVD cases as he walks toward the shelf. With every title, his mind's eye floods with memories of watching each one with his father. Jurassic Park, where his father explained the use of animatronics combined with computer-generated imagery to make the effects of dinosaurs come to life.

"Ahead of its time," he said, "and still unmatched." An image of the monstrous Kraken plays in his mind as he reads the spine for "Clash Of The Titans," where he first learned the term "stop-motion," and a lengthy biography of Ray Harryhausen, pioneer of that type of animation.

He had never seen his father so excited about a subject. The titles string together as he kneels to the bottom shelf. A collection of films and a documentary about stop-motion animators,

"The Brothers Quay," a demonstration film from the early days of CGI, and finally, *The Nightmare Before Christmas* on the second-to-bottom shelf. A line in the dust in front of the DVD box confesses a secret and is a window into his brother's pain. He knows his brother misses his father but has never considered how deeply an eight-year-old can feel such loss.

He just wanted to watch a Halloween movie at Halloween time, David reasoned. Yet, Ethan had been ready to walk into this room before his older brother was ready. How? Perhaps his little brain can't feel as nostalgic as an adult's and does not feel the same sorrow.

Or maybe I'm not going to heal as quickly as I hoped? Or maybe Ethan, as young and as short as his time has been, feels the loss on a greater scale? Is that possible?

"I'm hungry," Ethan calls from the other room.

"On it," David yells as he slides out the DVD. He walks towards the entrance with his gaze aimed at the exit, but stops when he sees his father's costume trunk behind the open door in the corner of the room.

He armpits the DVD and opens the trunk. A heavy rubber smell assaults his nose, equally strange and welcoming. Yellow, red, and purple eyes stare up at him from within. He rumbles through the trunk and pulls out a sea creature with dark green scales whose shape resembles his mother's, a goblin with purple skin whose face resembles Ethan's, and a vampire with elongated teeth and pale skin covered with blood. Out of all the masks, this one looked the most "human." His father spent more time than usual airbrushing the skin to make it look realistic. He returns the others to the trunk and throws the vampire mask resembling his father onto his bed.

A half-hour later, the sun has set, and the food is cooked. David hands Ethan a bowl and starts the movie. The narrator explains that realms exist for each holiday to live when they are not bringing their celebrations to Earth. A jack-o'-lantern door carved into a tree opens, and the camera swoops in. The violin strings from the opening number "This Is Halloween" fill David with bittersweet nostalgia.

Each monstrous denizen of Halloween town introduces itself: the thing "hiding under your bed," the thing "hiding under the stairs." Finally, Jack Skellington, the "Pumpkin King," emerges. When he was ten, he had shuffled close to his father when they first watched the film, not knowing if it was a kid's movie or if his father was trying to scare him.

He looks over at Ethan, frantically forking his mac into his mouth as his eyes are glued to the screen. It took David a while to understand that even though the monsters looked like monsters, they all worked to bring children joy, to celebrate death by normalizing death's role in life. Ethan shuffles closer to David without taking his eyes off the screen. The tiny action causes a lump to form in David's throat.

Maybe Ethan is more mature than I was at that age?

If that's so, he could be wrong about Ethan not feeling the loss as deeply. Yet, his younger brother continues to smile while David cannot avoid his father's absence. Not at Halloween. He does not want to muster up the mental fortitude to deal with that particular brand of sadness after such a long day, so instead of fighting off the memory, he embraces it.

"You know the shot with the bats coming up? Look above them this time, not at them."

The boogeyman's shadow on the moon smiles and stretches wide until it disappears, replaced by a horde of bats flying at the camera.

"They're on strings!" Ethan says, a noodle falling from his lips back into the bowl.

"Yep! We don't have the remastered version, so you can still see the strings holding them up."

"There's another virgin?" Ethan's brow furrows. David tries not to laugh at his speech blunder.

"It's the same movie, but they cleaned it up so it looks newer. Because they are all puppets, someone is behind them moving them and taking pictures one shot at a time to make it look like they're moving."

"That's the stuff Dad did?"

"Yep. Stop-motion, it's called."

"Why can't we see the strings?"

"Someone erases them."

Ethan takes in this information and then nods as though he is done processing.

"I like seeing the strings," he says. "It makes it more real."

"Me too," David laughs. "Dad, too. He likes seeing how things work. How things that aren't alive are brought to life."

"Is that why you are working at the haunted farm?"

David is surprised by the insightful question. "Yeah, it's like being a part of a movie, but since I get to set up the things that scare people, it's like I'm the monster."

"Does that mean you're the Pumpkin King now?"

"I guess it does," he smiles.

"I want to be the Pumpkin King," he whines.

"One day, little man."

A metal screech fills the room, and the front door pops open, prompting a gasp from the brothers. David squeezes Ethan and sits up straight. Tracy's wide eyes stare at them from the doorway.

"I'm so sorry," she laughs.

"Don't laugh," David says.

"You got weirded out by me knocking yesterday, so I didn't."

"It's fine, but you scared the hell out of us."

"Bad word," Ethan says.

"Sorry, but it's true."

Ethan considers this and nods his head in agreement.

"I didn't mean to interrupt. I'll see you tomorrow." She pulls the door, but David stands up and protests.

"You don't have to go."

"David," Ethan whines.

"It's okay," she says, but her face is full of contemplation.

"You okay?" David asks.

"Yeah," she says, unconvincingly. "We can talk tomorrow."

"No, talk to me." He walks around the table and motions towards his bedroom.

"David," Ethan whines louder.

"It's okay, I'll be right out," he tells his brother.

"Can she watch it with us?" Ethan asks, voice full of hope.

"I'd love to," she says, "if it's okay with you guys."

"I can make some popcorn after we talk," David offers.

"I can't have any this late," Ethan whines. "Mom says."

"I won't tell her if you don't," David says with an air of mischief.

Ethan rapidly nods his head.

"Keep the movie on," he tells Ethan. "We'll be right back."

David follows her into his bedroom and shuts the door. She sits on the bed, and he can tell by the way she places her hands on the counter and looks at the floor that she's inebriated.

"Did you drive here?" David asks.

"Of course not, I walked."

"I'm surprised you found it."

"David," she says as she shakes her head. "I've been walking to the house since we were in middle school." The way she talks holds more than just drunken haze.

"Tracy, what's going on?"

She looks up and into the darkness in the room, scrunching her nose like she has smelled something terrible. He sits next to her and clicks the light on the lamp on his nightstand.

"This looks like your dad," she says, picking up the mask from his bed.

"What better mask to wear to a Halloween party than one modeled after a murderer?"

She gives him a disapproving stare, which he still finds cute despite her stupor. "Manslaughter, not murder, and he's innocent," which she slurs as "in-cent."

"I guess that doesn't matter now," he says, taking the mask from her hands and throwing it on the floor. "What did you want to talk about?"

Tracy leans forward and kisses him on the lips. David freezes as her lips linger, her eyes close. He does not know why she is doing this but imagines that whatever is causing her to drink on a weeknight, presumably alone, is the culprit. Still, where his mind hesitates, his body reacts. He returns the pressure on her lips, gently at first, offering her the option for approval or retreat.

Her lips part, and she slides her tongue into his mouth. Thoughts escape him as a rush of adrenaline takes over, and they continue to kiss as they collapse onto the bed. His body reacts, offering its approval against her thigh. He pulls his hips back, but she closes the space with hers to accept his body's proposal. The moment of embarrassment has been enough to capture his attention away from what is happening.

"Tracy, what is going on?"

"I don't know," she says, rubbing a hand through his curls while trying to kiss him.

"You're drunk," he says.

"I know what I'm doing," she says, and then kisses him more. The kiss feels so good that he does not want to stop.

"Are you sure?" he asks.

"I wasn't drunk when I wanted to do this yesterday, or the day before."

"How long have you... I didn't know you liked me."

"I don't want to lose you," she says, and tries to kiss him again, but he pulls back.

"I'm not going anywhere."

Her eyes narrow, and her face hardens. "You should. You should share this with the world."

She looks around the room, and he knows she's talking about his work.

"I'm not that good," he says, feeling the sting of reality.

"You can be," she says, and then moves her body against his to force him to lie on the bed. She straddles his waist and continues to kiss him, then sits up to pull her shirt off. She reaches back to unclasp her white bra. The bedroom door opens.

David sits up. Tracy lets go of her clasp and holds her arms against her chest to cover her cleavage.

"Tracy, please leave so I can talk to my son," David's mother says.

"I'm sorry," Tracy says as she hurries to pick up her shirt from the floor.

"Mom, I'm nineteen," David reasons. "You even left me—"

"All I asked is that you spend time with your brother."

"It's my fault," Tracy says. "I was just—"

"Do you need a ride home?" his mother asks Tracy, her expression not giving away disapproval.

"I can walk," Tracy answers, and then slips past his mother, giving David a worried look before leaving. David sits at the edge of the bed as his mother continues to stare at him with cold eyes. He stands and walks towards the door.

"Where do you think you're going?"

"To sit with Ethan."

"I'll switch shifts with someone for tonight. It probably means I'll need to work a double this weekend."

"You don't need—"

"If I hadn't forgotten my purse, would I have found him alone on the couch in the morning?"

David stays silent. His mother closes his door as she leaves.

His mind and body flood with so many conflicting emotions that he ends up collapsing into his desk chair and sobbing. He almost lost his virginity to his best friend, but doesn't know if that would have been a good decision, since the moment felt so sudden. And what was bothering Tracy so much that she needed to come over and spill... what was it?

A crush? Love? Why would she feel anything for him other than friendship when that is all they ever shared? Did she want more from him? Does he want more from her? He had never considered her that way. He was about to have more, if not interrupted. His mother told him to make good decisions, but he took no time diving headfirst into a situation he had never considered. Just like his father.

David slams his fist on his desk. He looks around the room at the drawings and photographs he has created, which Tracy implied might be worth a buy-in for a productive future. He slams his fist on the desk again. Crushes, sex, dream jobs, creativity, a future - none of it mattered. His mother can't do it alone. When presented with that decision, his father placed his family above his desires, so if David didn't do that, what was he worth?

"Grow up," he says.

...but don't put your shoes exactly in his footprints.

He turns on his computer and waits for the screen to illuminate. He opens the terminal window and enters a prompt that opens a private browser window. He types the URL he memorized so that he does not risk bookmarking the link to the video on the dark web. A four-by-three video appears in the middle of a blank page.

A man in a red hard hat walks from the right side of a large warehouse towards a metal rack holding shelves full of textiles on the left. He presses one of two large buttons on a rectangular remote sitting next to the rack. The shelves descend, circulating levels of textiles so they can be easily retrieved. Gears are heard grinding, followed by a snap. One by one, the metal frame that holds the racks separates and falls forward, sending a cascade of metal and ceramic to crush the man before he has time to back away.

The sound his body makes still keeps David awake at night. He closes the browser window and stares at the mask lying on his floor.

CHAPTER 6

WEDNESDAY, OCTOBER 29TH

GABE IS CLIPPING HIS walkie onto a leather tool belt as David enters the communications room. "One of the barn cameras shifted. Frequency two. I'll call you when I get there."

"No problem," he says, and offers Gabe the second cup of coffee with "Luke" written on the side. Gabe takes it and walks out of the room without acknowledging the nicety. David is used to Gabe's distracted mind, so he doesn't take offense.

He sits in the leather chair and stares at the flat screen monitor with the eight video feeds, one of which shows the inside of the wall of the barn instead of the interior. His mind wanders as he waits for further instructions, unable to let go of the memory of Tracy on top of him. How nice it was for his body, and how confusing it was, and is, for his mind.

The radio crackles. "Good morning, by the way," Gabe says. "Sorry. I'm just anxious to get this done and get on the road. Thanks for the coffee."

"No problem, man," David laughs. "Good morning."

He watches the monitors, and as he waits for Gabe's instruction, he pulls out his phone and texts Tracy: *Can we talk?*

He stares at the screen and waits for her to reply.

The walkie crackles. "Looks like something hit it, probably a bird," Gabe says.

David looks at the monitor to see the ground view shifting to show a fisheye distortion of Gabe's face filling the screen.

"Don't look at my bats this time."

David laughs, "Was that a joke, Gabe?"

"You don't know me well enough to make fun of me, David."

"I'm sorry, man."

"That was a joke, David."

"Well done," he laughs again. He pushes a button on the switchboard to fill the screen with the one feed. The audio pops through the speaker on the desk. "I hear you through the monitor if you need both hands," David confirms through the walkie.

"Perfect," Gabe says through the camera. David can see him clip the radio onto his belt then continue adjusting something on the camera. "Video clear?" He leans back and waits for David's answer. Besides the glare from the window in the loft behind Gabe, the image is clear.

"Crystal," David speaks into the walkie.

"I'll drop off the walkie, and then I'm headed out. You got the helm."

"Aye-aye, Captain."

Gabe toasts him through the camera with the coffee and gives a thumbs-up. He leans forward, and the image on the monitor rotates to where the tractor and trailer will park during the event. David's phone vibrates in his hand.

We don't have to. I was drunk and sad. I'm sorry.

He feels a twinge of disappointment because even though he has never had romantic feelings for Tracy, it's nice to think someone smart and attractive has feelings for him. Someone who sees him in a positive light despite knowing everything about him; his faults and insecurities. His father, from before and after the incident that changed their lives. If at least one person can separate him from that moment, maybe a better future than he imagined is possible.

Why sad? He replies. A screech from the desk speaker pulls his attention to the monitor.

"I don't care..." he hears a man's voice yelling.

"Maybe you should," another voice replies. It sounds like Gabe's, but David has never heard Gabe raise his voice beyond his soft tone. "What's going to happen is going to be on your conscience."

David leans on the desk as though his proximity will make the sound clearer. The image on screen shows Gabe's shoulder peeking from the bottom of the screen. Whoever is with him is standing under the loft and behind its post.

"It's all under control. What are you so worried about?"

"If it's under control, then why do you care where it is?"

"I need to make sure she didn't tell anyone."

"I'm leaving. Whatever happens on Friday is not on me. Get out of my way."

The sound of shuffling feet.

"Give it to me, Gabe."

More shuffling feet.

"Get off of me."

David clicks on the alternative shot, which shows the view from the right of the entrance. Only Gabe's shoulder can be seen from behind one of the loft's pillars.

"Give it to me and I'll let you leave," the other man shouts.

"Get—" Gabe yells and unleashes a guttural noise that sounds less like aggression and more like surprise... or pain.

"Gabe, what's going on?" David asks through the walkie, but doesn't get a response, nor does he hear the radio squawk from the desk speaker. Gabe must have turned it off to preserve the battery. He tries other channels, but none are on to receive a signal.

Are you near the barn? he texts to Tracy. He notices the three dots are still active but then disappear as his text is sent. The dots return, followed by a reply: *I'm at the morning meeting. We can talk about it later.*

He can be at the barn quicker than he can explain what is happening through text, so he rushes out of the communications bunker, runs between the dormant bonfires, and through the carnival grounds of workers, rides, and game booths. He bounds through the thick rows of cornstalks until he passes through the other side and into the forest. He approaches from the right exit, calls out Gabe's name, and waits for a response. After a few seconds, he walks inside. The barn is empty.

"Gabe?"

Shuffling from outside catches his attention. He hurries out and runs to the back, but does not see the person who caused the sound. The forest is thick and already rustling with the wind. Whoever has come through is already gone. A shriek erupts on his right. He yells out of surprise and falls back against the barn.

"Earhart, where are you?" John says through the walkie-talkie.

David waits for his heart to stop pounding before he attempts to speak. He unclips the walkie from his belt and lifts it. He clicks the talk button but loses his words as he sees two rows of divots in the dirt path leading into the back edge of the forest.

"I'm here."

"Have we placed all the cameras?"

"Gabe had to fix one, but he... disappeared?"

"Yeah, he does that," John says.

"He's the king of the Irish goodbye," Kevin laughs through the walkie.

"I can vouch for that," Ryan offers.

But David's thoughts hardly acknowledge the others' words. He cannot keep his imagination from following the trail, nor can he pull his eyes from the darker spots sprinkled throughout the dirt. He lifts the walkie to protest their conviction, but thinks better of arguing. Someone was arguing with him, attacked him, or at least had a scuffle. If Gabe has a problem with someone, it wasn't David's place to communicate that information to everyone.

"Yeah," David replies. "I think he left. I'll check the cameras at HQ one more time, but we should be good to go."

David walks inside the barn. Something happened here. Whether Gabe is in danger or has been involved in a spat between young men that ended in a few shoves, he doesn't know.

The coffee cup with his father's name on it lies in the middle of the room, surrounded by its spill. Even in the few weeks that David has been on the job, he has never known Gabe not to finish a cup of coffee. But that is all he knows about Gabe. None of what these people do makes much sense.

"Great," John's sigh comes through the walkie. "Don't worry about Gabe. I'm sure he'll be happier where he's going."

David walks back through the cornfield and into the fairgrounds. None of the carnival workers' pay him any mind as he snakes through the game tents, food booths, and rides. The smell of weed permeates the air, and he wonders how much everyone gets away with being in the middle of nowhere, without authority. An annoying thought, because even though he is supposed to be an adult, he yearns for another adult, an older adult or someone mature, to tell him he's safe.

He looks towards the east, where Lillian's house stands atop a hill, looking down at everything she owns. David had once waited in line for the haunted maze while his father pointed at the three-story, looming house on a hill and called it the "Psycho House." He hadn't been old enough to see the movie or understand the reference, but that didn't stop his father from telling him to look through the upper-left window to see a woman's shadow.

"Don't ever go in there," his father said with his telling, teasing smile. "Or she will get you."

Even though he knew his father was kidding, his preteen mind raced with deadly possibilities... until he turned eleven and watched the movie.

David had no idea why his mother protested his father showing it to him, as he found the movie boring and didn't understand how anyone could stay awake during a movie that had no color. That broke any dire fantasy he had about the "Psycho House," and every following Halloween, he had to pretend to be intrigued by his father's insistence on calling it that. However, the more horror he watched and the older he became, the more curious he became about the genre.

One October night at age fourteen, he grabbed the Blu-ray from an Alfred Hitchcock remastered collection he had gifted to his father for his birthday and watched it from beginning to end. The movie was scary, but scary in a new way than he had previously understood. Murder was not the terror driving the narrative—moral ambiguity, unrequited love, gender differences, and dysphoria. The full range of human strife on display helped him understand the complexities of the genre, reinvigorating his fascination with it while also re-contextualizing the conversations with his father about why he studied to be an artist and filmmaker. Even though the house was no longer "scary," it was still a source of wild speculation and imagination.

The people meeting in that house are in charge, and they seem to be as self-involved and immature as he considers himself to be. He remembers his father's musing about knowing how life works. "When the magic is gone, all that is left is reality, and sometimes that is very, very disappointing." He returns to the communications building and finds Kyra leaning against the switchboard.

"Hey, Shaggy."

"Oh, hey." He fails to act casually. "Is the meeting over?"

"No, but I know what it's about. John has an announcement."

"I know, Lillian told me."

"Yeah, I've known for a while. I wanted to get some things done before everyone started bugging me for things. You're on your own now," she says, her smile full of mischief. "Scared?"

"I don't think Gabe is a person who would have left without ensuring that what he left would run smoothly."

"Why do you do that?" she asks, her voice dropping several octaves.

"Do what?"

"Refuse to give yourself credit."

David doesn't know how to answer that, so he shrugs.

"I just hate when people act weak." She rolls her eyes. Her word choice hits him like a brick to the chest.

"You think I'm weak?"

"The men in my life don't give up," she shrugs.

His father also told him about egos and agendas. There's a difference between a person wanting you to know your story versus a person wanting to absorb your story to strengthen theirs. "Is that what I am? A man in your life?"

She looks at him as though he has hurt her feelings. "Would you like to be?"

"I guess I don't know what that means."

Her smile returns, that sly curl of lips that says she is about to devour him, for better and worse. "I guess we will have to see." She straightens and turns around but stops. Her playful attitude lessens, and she looks at the floor.

"I do like you. You're kind, talented, and you're not a part of this cesspool. I don't know if I'm up for anything serious, but I'm curious to see where this goes." She leaves the room, and he sits there until he hears the front door shut.

He rolls back to the desk on shaky legs. His mind drifts to Tracy and whether pursuing a relationship would be fair to her if there is a prospect of starting one with Kyra. He imagines himself at the farm next year, working with Kyra while creating an amazing theme park. Unlike his parents, they will share the same ambitions and hobbies. They could pursue their dreams of a career and a relationship together. He went from his friend kissing him to a woman he has a crush on telling him there is a possibility of them getting together. All good problems to have, he thinks...

...but neither is a possibility when he has a family to help support. *A relationship?* He sighs. *A career? I haven't even applied to college yet.*

"I'm not ready for this," he says aloud. He also can't help but think it's all too good to be true.

On the feed that shows the barn floor, the coffee cup—the one that no one could have known about, and no one was around to pick up—is gone. He pulls out his phone and texts Tracy: *Is there anyone not at the meeting who's normally there?*

Her reply comes immediately: *Dougie is late as usual, but other than him, I don't think so.*

Except for Kyra, he feels like texting, and wonders why Tracy didn't mention her absence.

Why?

He doesn't know how to answer her. Instead, he thinks about last night's conversation with his brother. "Behind every puppet is someone pulling the strings," he told Ethan.

"Why can't we see the strings?" A smart question. His answer echoes through his mind, but instead of fading, it amplifies.

CHAPTER 7

"ONE FRIGHT ONLY" SHINES brighter as the sun sets, its green fluorescence mixing with the pink autumn sky. The colors remind David of the schlocky horror comics his father used to bring home from the liquor store on his way home from work on Friday nights.

The same hues that artist Tim Jacobus used to illustrate the covers of the R.L. Stine Goosebumps series from the early nineties, the first books he read. Every year, on the days leading up to Halloween, David asks himself if he "feels" the spirit of the holiday enough to celebrate properly. Had he watched enough of his favorite Halloween movies? Had he read a new horror book? Had he done enough spooky activities?

Traditions. Celebrations. Nostalgia. That feeling had been his fuel for happiness. Without his father to celebrate, he resolved to leave the expectation of those feelings, because they are a child's feelings, not the reality of an adult. And yet, the Halloween spirit has grasped him, maybe more than ever. And he's not just a passive participant. He is part of it. That joy, that specific nostalgic joy, has returned.

His father is not here. His life has changed. Yet, joy lives on. Shame jump-scares him out of nowhere and wrestles with that joy. Life should not be allowed to move on this easily.

Two large pyres blaze beyond the farm's opening gates, throwing dancing shadows across the park. He stands between them to be engulfed in their heat.

"Newbies in the back, Earhart," Mark commands as he nearly hits David in the head with a wooden bench before dropping it between the bonfires. David steps away from the fire and feels cold air on his back, reminding him of roasting marshmallows. He smiles. He can't help it. Not even bullies can kill his Halloween.

"He's an honored guest tonight," a voice calls out from beyond the flames and the crackle of burning wood. Kyra moves into the light between the pyres. The fire reflects off her pale skin, and the shadows they create accentuate her curves. She is wearing a red Victorian-style dress that covers her feet, the hem already stained with mud from walking across the farm.

Puffy cuffs wrap around her upper arms to leave her shoulders bare save for the thin straps of a red bra that push her breasts up to accentuate her cleavage. Her black hair is pulled up into a bun and held in place by a bloody dagger. Tinier versions of the dagger hang from her ears, stained with the same red as her dress, their blades reaching down to her clavicles.

Mark has stopped moving to watch her entrance. He looks at David and shakes his head.

"Don't be jealous," he throws at Mark with a wicked smile. His sudden candor comes as a surprise, and he wonders if it's because he's thinking with a brain full of hormones or if he has found strength in Kyra's acceptance. Or her protection. Mark's expression drops.

"You'll learn," he says and then walks away.

I'm sure I will.

He is not so full of himself to consider that he is just "flavor of the week" for a strong-willed woman, but there is a scrap of hope that whatever she sees in him, besides pity, is the same quality he sees in her. She walks with her head held high, not just because she's beautiful, but because she can run circles around this place without breaking a sweat, which is most likely why she has been chosen to take on the reins of such an event at a young age. She seems more adult than the rest.

What made her grow up so fast? No, that's not the right question.

Getting older is inevitable. Time will pass, and all someone has to do is the bare minimum to get to the other side of aging. The real question is, what made her grow up so fast and still be able to handle it all?

"Elizabeth Bathory, I presume?"

She curtsies. "You look underdressed for this dark engagement," she says.

"I was about to go change," he nods towards the communication shed.

"Can't wait to see what mask you put on," she winks and holds out her red-velvet-gloved hand. "Help a lady up?" She nods towards the bench and lifts the megaphone she is holding in her other gloved hand.

"Of course," he smiles, then lifts her arm around his back. He grabs her waist to support her, and parts of him grow attentive without his consent. He curses the remnants of his post-pubescent mind and wonders if his body will grow past that reaction. He does not wish to sexualize a woman he's trying to support, even if that support is physical.

"Good thing I decided not to wear heels," she says as she steps onto the bench with her sneakers. She plants both feet down and releases her grip from his shoulders, but her body wavers under the teetering bench. David grabs her hand and holds her steady, as her other hand lifts the megaphone and amplifies her voice across the fairground.

"Gather 'round, as we kick off our annual dark ritual!"

Kevin walks out of the north cornfield with Ryan, Pam, and a few older workers in tow, carrying bags of hot dogs, buns, drinks, marshmallows, and other food supplies. Dougie exits the haunted house with a few of the workers who are closer to his age.

"This year our frights spread from this humble farm to the internet, and will bring in a breadth of victims from across the country. First New Jersey, then the world!"

The crowd cheers, except for Ryan, who has not stopped giving David the most terrifying stare he has ever received. David lets go of Kyra's hand, but she teeters on the bench and places her hand on his shoulder for balance. He pretends not to see Ryan's face as it continues to burn a hole in his soul... and tries his best not to smile.

"Keep up the incredible work and prepare for a night you will never forget!"

The crowd cheers again. David can't take his eyes off her beaming, confident face. Kyra places the megaphone on the bench and grabs David's other shoulder. He wraps his hands around her waist and lowers her to the dirt, ensuring the dress doesn't get caught under her feet.

"Which night were you referring to?" David asks. "Tonight, or Halloween?"

Kyra smiles knowingly. Mischievously. "I guess that depends on your expectations."

"What should I be expecting?" he asks, mirroring her contagious smile. She lifts an eyebrow and taps him on the nose like a toddler. "Go get your mask and get a drink. We'll hook up later."

She turns around and walks between the fires before he has the wherewithal to ask if she meant "hook-up" in the sense that he hopes.

He returns to the communication room to grab a torn jacket and the vampire mask from his laptop bag. He puts them on as he returns to the fairground, grabs a beer from one of the engineers passing them out, and then sits on the same bench between the fires. The eerie stings of a theremin mix with laughter to permeate the night, held aloft by a backbeat of crackling wood and bass guitar. The amusement area is filled with nearly three dozen ride maintenance workers, carnival game barkers, and the fright crew.

Most of them remain unidentifiable under makeup and costumes. Most are lazily wearing that year's pumpkin costume.

Some adorn store-bought icons, like Ghostface, Michael Myers, and Freddy Krueger. Some are knock-offs, but the effort has been made. David is sure the three people he saw wearing hockey masks bought them at a sports store instead of a costume shop, but at least they are trying.

This is what David loves most of all about Halloween. All ages, all races, celebrating a holiday that mixes several religions and traditions from the beginning of humankind. All of them hiding under a mask, their unique expressions of fun that still equalize them in their creativity and bring them together. He laughs at the thought, lifting the beer in his hand and regarding the bottle through the small circles in the mask. Having only been drunk once in his life, and buzzed only on two occasions, he thinks he has just realized the kind of "drunk" he is going to be: the philosophical one.

"Better than an angry one," he says.

"Excuse me?" The thirty-something woman sitting on the bench beside him turns her head away from the man's face she had been tonguing. He hadn't realized he had spoken.

"Not you, sorry." He lifts the bottle in a salute. The woman laughs and returns to her infiltration of the other man's mouth.

"The plot thickens," Dougie says as he squeezes between David and the couple. He is wearing a long black coat and has his blonde hair sprayed black to resemble a character from The Matrix.

"Excuse me?" the woman says as she comes up for air. The man she is tonguing continues to look past her and at the fire in a stupor.

"Y'all want a third?" Dougie asks the woman. She rolls her eyes and pulls on the man's shirt to lift him off the bench and away from the fire. Dougie offers David an open beer, which he is about to drink until he thinks better of it.

"You didn't piss in this, did you?"

"If I were going to prank you, I would have resealed the cap to sell it better."

David drinks it. "You were saying something about a plot?"

"Kyra and you are a thing now," Dougie says.

"No. Maybe. It doesn't matter."

"Why doesn't it matter? You would have killed to have a girl that hot even look at you in high school."

"I'm not in high school anymore."

"Yes, I know," Dougie chides. "You're an adult. A family to take care of. I get it."

"What's with the sarcasm from you lately?"

Dougie laughs, but the sound is anything but joyous.

"I'm serious, talk to me." Whether it's the alcohol or his frustration with Dougie, he decides to be blunt. "You've been acting like you're on the defensive these days, and I don't know what it is."

Dougie takes a sip and stares at the fire. The spray in his hair turns the sweat on the side of his face black as it traces around his ear and down his neck.

"I'm jealous."

"Of Kyra? Nothing has happened, and I don't think it will."

"No, something has happened," he says. David is confused until the subtext hits him like a brick in the chest.

"You mean Tracy."

"She said you kissed."

"Yeah, for like, thirty seconds."

"She said, and I quote, it was 'really hot.'"

David's face flushes. *It was hot.*

"I didn't know you liked her, Dougie."

"Oh, I don't," he laughs, this time with genuine laughter. David's confusion with his friend grows to the point of frustration.

"Then what's there to be jealous about?"

Dougie takes another sip and leans away from the fire. He looks at David with distant eyes.

"The problem with high school," he says, "is that all anyone does is lie to each other. Not because we are bad or devious, but because we are so damn confused about ourselves and those around us that we are too afraid to share our true selves. I thought that would be over when I got into the real world."

The words mirror David's feelings and untie a knot in his stomach that has been pulling since taking the job. "It's like high school never ended for half of these people."

Dougie lets out a sardonic laugh. "And you don't know what is real or a rumor because they all secretly hate each other while also trying to fuck each other."

"And the stuff that might be true, everyone seems to ignore."

"That comes back around to my problem," Dougie says.

"What have you heard?"

"It's safer not knowing."

"Safer? That's a specific word choice."

Dougie shrugs. "I think the people around here are up to something weird, and I think you're in the middle of it."

"Can you be more vague?"

"I don't think Kyra wants you for your looks."

Anger rushes through David. "So, you are jealous."

"Not jealous, observant. Why is the hottest woman you've ever seen, who hardly knows you, suddenly into you? Is it the lack of a real job? No plans for a future? A murderer for a father?"

"What the fuck, Doug?"

"Don't get mad at me; I'm just pointing out what you're not seeing."

"Fine, she has an agenda. Probably to piss off her ex. I considered that."

"I don't think it's that simple."

"Since when do you talk in riddles?"

Dougie takes another swig, contemplative, as though he is considering an answer to what David considers a facetious question.

"I can't tell you right now, but the more I hear, the more I think you might be right about everyone here. It's not just immaturity; it's something else."

"I'm your best friend, Dougie. Why can't you tell me? Especially if you think I'm going to get hurt, too."

"You stumbled upon two beautiful women who are into you while I'm still trying to figure out..." His jaw steels and his eyes narrow on the fire. "Forget it."

"What are you trying to figure out?"

"What are you going to do about Tracy?"

"I never thought about Tracy that way. And yeah, I like Kyra. She's smart, confident, and gorgeous. That doesn't mean anything is going to happen between us. I have to concentrate on Mom and Ethan. Don't start drinking the Kool-Aid that is turning everyone else into children."

"Children?" Dougie looks at him for the first time in minutes, his expression full of contempt. "I think I'm the only one here not acting like a child, and if anyone here might have a problem with drinking, it will be the only one who is the son of an alcoholic." He stands and walks away from the bench.

Despite the anger boiling within him, David does not want to stop the conversation. "A child walks away, Doug," David calls. Dougie keeps walking, throwing a middle finger over his shoulder. David wants to rush after him, but can already feel the dizzying effects of the alcohol, which will only prove Dougie correct.

David finishes the beer and then lines up the bottle with the other two empties. He stands on unsteady legs and searches for his phone in his pockets. He finds that only forty-five minutes have passed since the party started at sundown and only twenty minutes since the sky became sunless. Tracy should be here by now, and if he is going to talk to her seriously, he needs to stop drinking. With Dougie mad at him, he'll need a ride home from her if he doesn't sober up, and his mind should be clear if they are talking about something serious.

David shoves the mask in his pocket and grabs a hot dog from a round picnic table beside a grill manned by a pumpkin-masked staff member with a beard so large it bunches the rubber and closes the eye holes. Despite being unable to see, he keeps grilling and singing along to a remixed "Monster Mash" as he knocks back his beer and drops it to the ground to clink against a pile of other empty bottles. The grill-master throws his spatula in the air, lets out a yell of celebration, and, despite his clear inebriation, turns around and catches it behind his back.

David bites his hot dog and pulls up the streaming app he linked to the Wi-Fi to view the camera feeds. Friday morning, he will make them live for everyone to tune in. Until then, he needs to ensure that it keeps broadcasting without interruption or interference. There are many cameras at each attraction, so he has to flick through each one. John and Lillian didn't want anyone in the haunted house because of the careful setup, so those images are dark.

However, he can tell by the static inside the faded black that the lack of image is due to darkness, which means it's working properly. The next set is the camera in the Burn Barn, also static, but with hints of light across the ground. The next set is the Mad Scientist's lab, and he is surprised that the image is bright. The perspective is yellow-tinted, and the shadows are thick. Service lights in case of an emergency. Their power comes from the same generator as the cameras, so he will have to go turn them off to reduce the risk of the generator depleting.

He opens Tracy's text log.

Are you coming? He takes a picture of the stack of hot dogs and sends it to her.

I wasn't going to until you sent that! she replies. *JK. Pulling in now.*

Great! Headed to the lab to turn off some lights. See you soon. He sends her a ping using a Friend Finder app that will let her know his position then walks north through the corn until he hits the trail in front of the Burn Barn, checking that the entrance and exits are closed. He's pretty sure that morning he had witnessed an assault inside that place on someone he might not ever see again.

David makes his way down the trail and is happy that his inebriation is keeping his fear of being alone in the woods at bay. He tries not to look at the surrounding darkness and instead concentrates on the yellow emergency light coming from the lab's high windows. The light cuts as someone walks around the interior. The trailer door is open as he approaches, and he can see the silhouette of someone sitting on one of the surgery tables. He knocks on the wall and says, "Don't be scared."

The silhouette yelps and turns around. A bottle drops to the floor and rolls across the ground while spilling its contents.

"Shaggy," Kyra exclaims.

"I said, Don't be scared," he laughs.

"What are you doing here?" she asks, turning around and pulling her fluffy dress over to hang off the side facing him.

"I saw the service light on through the feed. I didn't want the generator's battery to drain."

"You really are good at your job," she says, pulling a half-filled six-pack of beer from around her, placing it at her side. "Care to join me?"

"I don't want to interrupt. If you were meeting with someone, I mean." He feels a shred of jealousy at the notion and regrets saying anything out of fear of her answer.

"What if I was waiting for you?" she says, feigning a flirtation that borders on mischief. She holds up a beer. "Maybe I turned on the light, knowing you would come and fix it?"

"That would require you to have a lot more faith in me than I do." He walks into the room and grabs the bottle. She offers him a bottle opener attached to a set of keys, and he uses it as he hops onto the table.

"And yet, you're here. Making sure everything is running smoothly."

David shrugs. "I guess."

"Attention to detail. Good work ethic. Be proud of yourself."

"I don't think I've been working long enough to develop a work ethic."

"Maybe it's hereditary?"

"Hereditary," he laughs. "You know what my father did."

They each take a swig and let the distant sound of music fill the space. David looks at the bottle and reminds himself that it is the same substance that compromised his father's judgment, ending in gross negligence and death. He takes another swig and feels the guilt slide down his throat and into his stomach, where he carries all of his emotions.

She looks at him without humor. "When you interviewed, Lillian had me do some research. I watched the old news reports.

I read the case reports. I even read the social media keyboard warriors with their dumb hot takes. I don't think your father was negligent. Drunk at the time, maybe, but I think his boss was lying about those emails."

"How can you be so sure? You don't even know him."

"I have a sixth sense about people, especially with liars." She takes a swig without breaking eye contact. "His boss was lying."

"I appreciate that," he says, and means it even though her words make him angry. It's easier to think that his father was lying and got caught, rather than being innocent and suffering. He tries to change the conversation. "If you're not meeting anyone, what are you doing here?"

"Despite the rumors around here, I like being alone."

"Do you want me to go?" he asks, again afraid of the answer.

"I also like being with you," she says. "So, no, you can stay."

"Why?" He realizes he might be the type of drunk who doesn't know how to shut his mouth.

"How badly do you want to fuck me, David?"

His heart skips a beat, and he flounders with a response. "What?"

She sets her beer next to her. "You said you did community theater and high school drama. You know what it's like working closely with other people your age, creating something together. There is a passion and intimacy in that environment. This environment. So when I tell you that most of the rumors about me... well, everyone here, are true, you understand the context."

"I do." He remembers his own experiences in those situations, the excitement of putting on a show, and how that provided opportunities to hook up with actresses and stagehands behind the scenes. "I don't judge you, Kyra. I'm not one of those people who call women sluts for liking sex while also praising their male friends for doing the same thing."

"Like I told you, I have a sixth sense about people. So, how badly do you want to fuck me?"

He takes a swig and then places the beer on the table. Although he's terrified, her candor gives him confidence. "You're one of, if not the most beautiful women I've ever known. You're also hard-working, smart, and confident. So yeah, I can't get the thought of you out of my mind."

"But?" she says, already leading on that she knows his answer.

"My life is complicated right now. I have a family to look out for, and after this job is over in two days, I need to spend my time finding another job and taking care of my brother when my mother works nights. I'm plowing through life day by day, terrified of my future, and I don't know what I have to offer someone. One or two nights of sex might lift my spirits, but it will only add to the stomach-full of emotions that I have not experienced. On the other hand, I like you, and if I spend the night with you, the conflicting emotions might literally make my body fall apart." He laughs at the absurdity of his word salad.

She tilts her head and smiles at him, her inebriation showing through her body language. "See? Ethics."

"So you like me only because I'm the only person who can resist jumping into your pants?"

"I'm not that much of a cliché, Shaggy." She places the tip of one of her long, red costume nails under his chin and pulls his face towards hers. "I like you because, out of everyone else around me, you know the show always comes first."

"The show?" he asks, realizing she might not be talking about the farm's attraction.

"It's all a show," she whispers, leaning her face closer. "A trial of personality. You know that better than anyone." She presses her lips against his, and he stiffens his lips to kiss her back.

"David?" another voice calls from the entrance.

He turns to see Tracy. The disappointment on her face makes David's heart sink.

"Tracy, I..." David says, but she is already out of sight.

"Go after her," Kyra says. "We can talk tomorrow."

"Are you sure?"

"Don't lose a friend over me."

"Thank you," he says, and then runs out of the lab to see Tracy running from the trail and into the woods. He runs after her, but he can't see which way she fled. After two minutes of seemingly endless darkness, he realizes he no longer knows if he is heading in her direction. Already tired from running earlier, he gasps for air and resigns to sitting in the dirt. He pulls out his phone and texts Tracy: *Let's talk about this. Please.*

His breath fogs the screen as he awaits a response. A few minutes later, he calls her. The line connects straight to her voicemail. After another minute, he tries again. Voicemail. David realizes she might have blocked his number, so he emails her the same message. The video feed app is still up, so he cycles through each view, hoping to see where she is. He stops swiping when he sees Dougie standing on the trail in front of the out-house, drinking a beer and carrying another under his armpit.

He is about to put his phone away when he sees a pump-kin-masked figure emerge from the stalks, making David react as though he is watching a jump scare from a horror movie. Dougie also jumps back, dropping both beers. David lets out a laugh and watches his friend catch his breath.

He can't hear the conversation but imagines Dougie is being ridiculed, most likely by Mark, since the outhouse is his "Scare Point." Since Tracy is already gone and Dougie is only half a field away, he might as well catch him and apologize. A minute and a half later, the top camera pole and the top of the outside appear through the slits in the stalks.

On the trail, Dougie is gone. The dropped bottles lie there, so he picks them up to throw them out. Next to them lies a cell phone. The blue case tells him it's Dougie's, and when he touches the screen to light it up, an illustration of an anime man in a suit and a katana glows as his wallpaper. At the bottom of the screen is a text notification from "Crush."

Sounds good. Meet you in a few minutes.

He pokes the text and is relieved that there is no lock. The message fills the screen, and the prompt for the reply reads: *Told mom I'm staying at David's. Meet me at the outhouse now so we can head out together.*

Would Dougie have asked him to stay if they hadn't argued, or was he just an excuse to spend the night with his "Crush?" He opens his mouth to call his friend's name, but hesitates. He could call Kyra on his cell and ask for help, but if Dougie had just pissed someone off and had an argument, would that make David look childish for butting in?

He swipes through the images again. No Dougie, no Tracy, and his concentration wanes under an inebriated mind. He also realizes that at some point, he has dropped his father's mask.

"Fuck!" he screams, knowing he is too drunk to drive and has no way to get home. He stumbles back to the lab, but Kyra is gone, the doors are closed, and no light emanates from the windows. He looks up the email he received from John listing everyone's contact information to find her number and then texts her: *Are you still here?*

No. Sorry. Getting away early. You okay?

Couldn't catch up with her. She was my ride. He responds.

Go to Lil's. She has sleeping bags for those who need to stay the night.

David looks up and sees the top of the house. A chill runs down his spine. He stumbles forward in its direction, stopping every so often until the pain from his growing headache and the dizziness pass enough to allow him to move again without throwing up. He moves around the Ferris wheel, through a crowd of drunken grown-ups and a few young adults, until he sees the house on the hill. A random thought pops in his head as he approaches it. *I did it, Dad. After all these years, I'm going into the 'Psycho House'!*

CHAPTER 8

THE HOUSE HAD LOOKED abandoned since the first time he laid eyes on it as a child, and now as he walks up the hill, more details of its rotting facade became apparent. The siding has not been repainted. The shutters are barely holding on, and the windows are caked with dirt. He feels a twinge of irony that the house used to look less derelict than it does now. Damn inviting.

He would have given anything to have a home this size instead of a one-story box. This place was a luxury. As for most of the situations he has been finding himself in these days, the reality is much less interesting than the fantasy he has built in his head, and a lot more complex. Why has Lillian let her home decay?

David knocks on the door but does not hear an answer for a few seconds. He moves to knock again but hears movement beyond the door. He thinks someone is approaching the door until he hears a man's voice invite him in from what sounds like far into the house. He opens the door and steps into a realm of heat that seems too egregious even with the autumn cold.

From the anteroom, he can see the kitchen ahead and a living room to his right, separated by stairs, littered with people in sleeping bags, some alone and some draped in half-clothed partners. The scene almost makes David laugh, resembling what he thought college would be in his mind, with what he heard about parties and promiscuity. He never believed any of it was as egregious as others have said, or what movies depicted, but this is damn close.

A pale figure crosses the entrance to the kitchen. David's heart jumps out of his chest, and he gasps. His eyes adjust to the dark enough to see Pam, wide-eyed and staring back at him. Her hair is disheveled, and a "Badger's Farm" shirt hangs down to her knees. She lifts a hand to wave at him and then proceeds to disappear through the other side of the kitchen.

Was Dougie here? He said they had a date that week, and that gives David hope that he didn't leave drunk and is in the house.

As he looks around the living room for an empty sleeping bag or a section of a couch, the interior confirms his observation that it has not been tended to, not because it is unkempt or dirty—quite the contrary—but because the wood flooring is scuffed and worn, and furniture in the living room is patterned with floral pastels on top of shaggy carpet, straight out of the seventies. Another creak from the kitchen pulls his attention. Pam returns with a bottle of water and a doughnut. She is met halfway across the entrance by another figure dressed in a black robe with red lining.

"John?" David asks, even though he recognized the man.

John looks at him with surprise. "David?"

"Hi. I... I was told there would be a place to sleep."

John looks around the room at the bodies lying on the floor. He leans down and says something to Pam that David can't hear. She nods slowly and then passes him as though she is barely paying attention.

"I have something much better for you," John says. "Follow me."

John leads him through the kitchen and up the stairs to the second floor. Each step creaks until he steps onto a shaggy carpet and is surrounded by pastel wallpaper. John walks ahead and enters the last door on the left. David walks down the narrow hallway, passing a room where he sees Pam lying on a bed with her doughnut in her mouth, her legs spread to reveal more than David is meant to see. He knows she is closer to his age than John, and wonders if that age gap is inappropriate. He tries not to dwell on it as he walks into the room John entered.

John is dropping a blanket and a pillow onto a small box-spring cot in the corner of the room. David looks around, and a surge of excitement breaks through his sickness. On the far wall in front of the window is a desk covered by a blueprint and a wooden model of a rollercoaster track. On the left wall is a shop bench with various tools and half-constructed models of a castle, an amusement ride cart, and sketches of ride layouts.

Every inch of the four walls is covered in charcoal sketches of monsters, decaying houses, nude men and women, and still-life images of pumpkins, street signs, and city skylines. David is so enamored with the creative cocoon that John's voice jump-scares him back to attention.

"How drunk and/or sober are you right now?" John asks.

"I think I'm more hungover," he says. "I've never drunk this much before, so I'm not sure." He regrets giving up that information, trying not to seem inexperienced, and failing.

"Well, I've been meaning to tell you this since Gabe left, and I have the energy now, so just let me know what you don't remember and I'll repeat myself in the morning." He talks fast and laughs at himself. David notices John's bloodshot eyes and erratic movements as he bends at the desk and opens a drawer. He's on something, but David's inexperience with different substances keeps him from guessing what that is. John pulls out a rolled-up paper held together by a rubber band and hands it to David.

"The area layout for each attraction. I'd like you to take a look and see if there are any blind spots for when we broadcast. Imagine you're an audience member following one person through the entire thing from start to finish. I want the audience to see her, even when we need to cut to another camera."

Like a final girl in a horror movie.

"Like the final girl in a horror movie," John says.

Excitement ignites within him, but then extinguishes when he realizes there are only two days to figure out and accomplish what John is asking.

"I'm not making an excuse, Sir, but Gabe didn't tell me that is what you needed, only to maintain what is there. I'm happy to do it, but I don't want to let you down."

John waves his hand in the air as he sits on a stool in front of a drafting desk. "This was never in the talks. I just want you to try..." he sighs and then takes a deep breath. "I'm planning something a little bigger, and I'd like to know how far I can take it. As you might have noticed, Gabe wasn't exactly the talkative type and had been more laconic than usual. It's hard to pitch ideas and collaborate with someone who is only comfortable with taking orders. Gabe knows that about himself. When he decided to move on, I asked him to be on the interview panel so we could find someone with more of an artistic eye, and not just a crew member, you know?"

David nods, trying to act humble without showing his emotions. Gabe and John saw him as an artistic person, not just a body who knew cameras. A fantasy plays out in his mind, of racing home at the end of the workday to tell his father of this amazing compliment.

"You want to make a prototype or something like a pilot episode that you can use as a proof of concept."

"I already have," John smiles. "I sold a pilot episode to a new streaming service and got a sizable advance to create a proper first episode."

"That's incredible. Congratulations. Is the idea about following a person through a haunted place?" He tries to keep his face stoic, professional, and not ecstatically giddy.

"Not exactly; it's about a person facing their fears. I interview a subject in a documentary-style format about their fears and phobias and then build a custom experience that allows them to face those fears."

"That's an awesome idea. It's like seeing where a person's fear is born and then watching them survive it."

"Exactly. I hope to hit the cross section between people who like documentaries and those who like game shows."

"That's why you're leaving?"

"I know it sounds like I'm betraying this place, but it's been a decade, and the farm isn't doing well. My attraction is the only thing keeping it afloat. There is barely enough money to maintain what I have been doing, let alone grow. I can't stay in one place and expect to grow. I'm not a plant."

He wonders if an opportunity like this could lead to more lucrative opportunities for him. If he does a good job, would John carry his name into his next endeavor?

"I know you've been through a lot, and I'd like to include people I know to help me get this off the ground. Kyra is already in, so are a few of the others. I think this will be a good opportunity for you to show your skills."

He opens his mouth to thank the man, but he can't use his voice without the risk of it cracking.

"I do want to apologize. Kyra told me what happened to your father, and I didn't know."

He closes his mouth before speaking again because he knows that his voice will crack. He tries to make light of the topic for both of them.

"I'm surprised. The video is everywhere. So was the case."

"Well, I might be an engineer, but my downtime is analog." He lifts his hands towards the many creations around the room. "I'm really sorry, David."

"I appreciate it," he holds the blueprint, "and the opportunity."

"Take that copy with you tomorrow. Look over it carefully and let me know if you see anything..." he trails off and thinks, "out of place." He slaps David on the arm and then walks out of the room.

David sits on the cot and places the blueprint on the floor. Excitement and adrenaline drown out the dizziness as he lies on the cot and stares at the fantastical drawings around the room. An incredible compliment. An opportunity for his future, not just in a creative field, but one that might also be lucrative, justifying his want to follow his dream and his need to support his family. His first instinct is to tell his father about the drawings, the man who drew them, and how he sees potential for his future.

Beyond the wall, he hears a bed squeak, followed by a woman's moan, which is most likely Pam. His excitement drops as he realizes that not only is Dougie not there, but the woman his friend is dating is sleeping with a man fifteen years older, who happens to be his new mentor. Was Pam not the 'Crush' Dougie had labeled in his phone? None of which is his business, nor his to judge, but like many situations that he has been in lately, he has no firm grasp of its truth or how he should feel about its implications.

He does his best to ignore the sounds and concentrate on the fact that, for the first time since his father's absence, he has hope for a positive future. He wants to tell someone. His mother, his brother, Tracy, Dougie... Kyra. If Kyra is going with them, and if the job pays...

He closes his eyes and thinks, *I made it into the 'Psycho House', Dad, and it's more than I have ever imagined!*

CHAPTER 9

THURSDAY, OCTOBER 30TH

DAVID PULLS BOTH PHONES out of his jeans before his eyes open. Neither Tracy nor his mother has replied. A merch shirt illustrated with this year's pumpkin mask design has been folded and placed outside the door, along with an unopened toothbrush and a travel-sized tube of toothpaste. The room John and Pam had occupied is open and empty, and he wonders if John is still in the house or already walking the grounds. The smells of toast and bacon rise from the stairway and make his queasy stomach growl, so he walks the hallway to find a bathroom, where he discovers Pam sitting on the floor and throwing up into the toilet.

"You okay?" he asks. Pam doesn't look up from the bowl, but gives a thumbs up before throwing up again. "Can I get you anything?" She turns her thumb down and then sits against the side of the tub, picking up a washcloth and wiping her mouth. Her eyes barely open, and her pale skin is somehow paler.

"Did I see you last night?" she croaks.

"Yeah," David blushes, not knowing if she knows how much of her he saw. "You were getting a doughnut."

She shakes her head and leans back towards the bowl to throw up once more, returning to her resting position when she finishes.

"I'll find another bathroom," he says. She shakes her head and waves towards the sink.

"Do what you gotta do."

The smell of her vomit makes David want to protest, but the quicker he acts, the sooner he can get downstairs to the smell of breakfast. He brushes his teeth, trying to ignore the sick woman who is staring at him in his peripheral vision.

"Thought you'd be spending the night with Kyra," she says slowly, as though any sudden movement will unleash another upchuck. With a mouth full of toothpaste, he has time to think through how he should reply. He considers his relationship with Kyra, not just between the two of them, but also how everyone views their correspondence from the outside. A twinge of anger coats his response.

Pam and he had never said more than two words to each other, yet she has an entire perspective and opinion on an aspect of his life that he still has no grasp on. Stories, rumors... entire movies about his life play in people's heads who hardly know him. They seem to have more input on his life than he does, which is aggravating and makes him aggravated with himself.

He spits into the sink. "I thought you were seeing Dougie?"

She tilts her head. "Dougie? Why would you think that?"

"Just what I heard."

"You did?" she smiles.

David's anger rises, but he knows she is most likely telling the truth. It wouldn't be the first time Dougie has lied about seeing a girl, but he thought that kind of immaturity would have been left behind in high school.

So much for "High School is over," eh, Dougie?

"Can I get you anything?" he asks before leaving the bathroom. She shakes her head and closes her eyes. David grabs his things and heads downstairs.

The kitchen and dining room are buzzing with over one dozen people making and eating breakfast. Lillian and Kevin are at the kitchen counter, flipping pancakes and bacon, laughing over something David didn't hear. Mark carries a carton of orange juice and milk into the dining room and places them in front of Ryan. As Ryan reaches for the orange juice, he notices David.

"Hey, new guy," Kevin says. David braces himself for a snide remark. Instead, he says, "Grab a plate and chomp down."

"Good morning, David," Lillian smiles. She is wearing a yellow apron that makes her appear older than her forty-eight years. "Didn't know you were staying with us last night."

"Me either," he says, grabbing a clean plate from the counter. "John set me up."

"I guess that means Kyra isn't far behind," says Kevin. "You'll have to make more chocolate chip pancakes," he tells Lillian and then points his spatula at David. "She likes her chocolate pancakes. Remember that."

With one of the senior staff members and one of the owners present, he might as well use this moment to set his record straight. "I'm not sure what everyone has heard, or if a rumor has gotten out of hand, but nothing is going on between me and Kyra. I hardly know her."

Lillian turns to give Kevin a stern expression. "This is what I've been talking about." She turns her head back to David and points her battered spatula at him. "Don't let these children get under your skin. If you want to keep things private, you don't owe anyone an explanation."

"Thank you, but I'm serious. Nothing is—"

"Are we getting more pancakes?" Ryan shouts from the other room.

"You can come in here and make your own," Kevin yells back.

David grabs a few pieces of bacon and two pancakes from the stacks on the counter and turns towards the dining room. He has no desire to deal with Mark and Ryan, and the living room is still littered with a few sleeping bodies.

"Ms. Badger, do you mind if I take this to communications? I want to make sure the cameras didn't get moved overnight."

"No problem, just bring the plate back later."

"Thanks," he says and walks towards the living room. He stops when he realizes he has something else in his pocket. "Did any of you see Dougie leave last night?"

Kevin looks at Lillian as though he is asking her for permission to speak.

"Not me," she answers.

"I saw him near the outhouse," David explains. "He dropped his phone. I'll give it to him when he gets in."

"I ran into him having a couple of drinks in the parking lot," Mark says, coming back into the room. "He said he's going to sleep in until rehearsal tonight."

"He lives near me. I'll drop it off on my way home tonight."

Mark looks at Lillian with the same stare Kevin had given her. Again, she shrugs, smiles, and looks at David. "No problem. I'll radio you if he comes back sooner."

"Why don't you come sit with us?" asks Mark. His offer seems sincere, and if David wants the chance to become accepted by the staff and earn their respect, this is as good a time as any. If he says "No", that could further the wedge between them.

"Sounds good," he says, and walks into the dining room. He takes the left head of the long table, away from Ryan in the middle, just in case. A few of the day workers he doesn't recognize are seated, and one or two sleepers from the living room take a seat to eat.

The scene reminds him of his family's Sundays, when his parents would make breakfast for the four of them, the smells of bacon and eggs, and the sounds of bubbling oil and the clinking of plates and utensils. No one would talk because everyone was still waking up, so his father would either play music or start a conversation about what everyone got into that week and what their hopes were for the week ahead. His father hated the silence and loved to hear everyone's stories.

Mark, Kevin, and Lillian have stopped cooking to set the remaining stacks of their labors on the table and sit to make their plates. No one says a word, and David realizes that if he's ever going to work with these people, even in the future, he needs to make a better impression rather than trying not to make a bad one.

"How's everyone feeling about rehearsal tonight?"

Mark, Kevin, Lillian, and Ryan look at him with mouths full of food. David deflates in his chair.

"I think it's going to be great," Mark offers.

"Just make sure you get it on camera," Kevin laughs, but it's not mocking.

"I got you covered," David laughs with him.

"Don't you have a little brother?" Lillian asks.

"Yeah."

"How old is he?"

"Eight."

"Does he like scary things?"

"Yeah, he's a lot like me."

"Invite him to the rehearsal tonight."

David thinks about that. It would be a way to smooth things over with his mother, save money on a babysitter, and provide a little fun for his brother. The only question is if he will be too scared to want to participate.

"I'll watch the feed for you," Ryan says, and it is the first time he has addressed David without saying something catty or derogatory.

"I want to make sure none of the effects affect the cameras, but I don't think he'd go on himself. Since Tracy is working the house, do you mind if she takes him on?" He immediately regrets offering Tracy as a volunteer, especially since he doesn't know if she will answer his call.

"Not at all," Lillian says. "It would be good to have a staff member on the ride."

"Don't trust me, David?" Ryan asks without looking, the side of his mouth curling into a smile. David has had his run-ins with bullies in high school, learning that they will keep coming for you unless you stand your ground.

"Only as far as I can throw you, Ryan, and as you can see, I don't play a lot of sports."

Kevin and Mark laugh, and to David's surprise, so does Ryan.

"I think I'm starting to like you, David."

"I'm still on the fence about you, Ryan."

"I'm still on the fence about Ryan, and I've known him for four years," Lillian says.

"I like to keep people on their toes," Ryan says with mock bravado.

"What is everyone laughing about?" Pam asks as she enters with an empty plate.

"Are you okay?" Kevin asks, picking up on her pale skin and drooping face.

"Hungover," she states.

"Among other things," Mark mumbles. Lillian gives him a look that makes him shrink in his chair. Everyone continues eating in awkward silence as she makes a plate and sits between Ryan and Lillian. She eats as if she has never tasted food.

"You're going to make yourself sicker," Lillian says. "I'll grab you some water and coffee."

Pam puts her fork down and leans her head back to rest on the back of the chair. David has finished his food and takes the plate into the kitchen. Lillian is pouring coffee from a pot into a mug as he places his plate and fork into the sink.

"Sorry about the awkwardness," Lillian whispers. "John doesn't care about the age difference. At least, not when they are younger." David assumes the history behind her words.

"I don't judge," David says. "Everybody has their thing."

"What's your thing?"

David thinks about that and then states the obvious. "My father's alcohol abuse led to someone's death."

"Well, technically, that's your father's thing. What's your thing?"

David leans against the counter and thinks about that. "That I'm going to become him."

"An alcoholic or a murderer?"

"Both," he says, but knows that's not true. "Neither." He continues to think about the question. "Honestly, it has nothing to do with that. I think he started drinking because he was sad that he gave up his dreams by getting my mother pregnant with me.

I'm scared of making a decision that will stop me, or that his decision to drink has already derailed my life."

"You think John is your way out?"

He is not prepared for that response, and its bluntness forces him to think about it.

"He is everything my dad wanted to be, and the person I want to be."

Lillian nods her head as she opens a sugar packet and pours it into the coffee.

"I can see that, but remember that one person has multiple sides," she nods her head towards the dining room, indicating John's involvement with Pam.

"You think I shouldn't work with him?" David asks.

"Not at all. Chase your dream and use anyone you can to get there. What I'm saying is that, if you respect John for one reason and push aside his flaws, you can do the same thing for your father."

David wants to protest because the anger towards his father over what he did and its aftermath still clouds his love.

"Thanks, but why bring it up?" he tries to deflect the conversation.

"My parents made a lot of terrible financial decisions when it came to this property and then worked themselves into heart attacks to leave me right on a sinking ship. The best I can do is keep heading in the right direction while bailing out as much water as possible."

David understands why she is telling him this. It's not about him, not entirely.

"That's why you put up with John, and," he mimics her nod towards the dining room, "he's one of the buckets helping you bail the water out."

"You get it," she says as she grabs a glass from a cupboard above the counter. David slides away from the sink to allow her to use the faucet.

"But why tell me?"

She fills the cup and turns off the faucet, then leans against the counter and sighs.

"I've worked with John for a long time, and despite his flaws, it's been an incredible partnership. So I mean no disrespect to him when I ask you this, but David, do you want to follow a man that will inevitably tank his career because of his flaws, or do you want to build something of your own and do it the right way?"

He hasn't seen John in the way she is projecting, so he can't argue with her viewpoint. He understands what she is asking of him, that if John is leaving, David might be staying here to build something of his own with them, which will allow him to stay close to his family as well. Yet, John has dreams that are a wider reach, on film, where David's heart is set.

"What does success look like to you?" she asks. "Fame? Fortune? Opportunity?"

"I never thought about it like that before," he says. What does he want? To create? To be known for creating? What legacy does he want to leave behind?

"Just think about it," she says, her somber face turning into a smile.

"I can see why they all look up to you," David says.

"I'm not able to have children of my own," she shrugs. "So I like to spread my wisdom to you disenfranchised youths."

"We appreciate it," David says.

Lillian walks back into the dining room. David grabs yesterday's clothes and the blueprint off the counter and thanks them all for breakfast. They all say goodbye. He leaves the house and turns around to look at it. So many feelings cross his mind that he can't make heads or tails of how he feels about the total experience of his first night in the "Psycho House". Like most experiences lately, he is left with a myriad of positive and negative emotions.

"Adulthood," he says aloud without meaning to. He looks over to the barn house down the hill to the south. Tracy is inside there, and although he wants to text her again, if he is going to save whatever is left of their friendship, he needs to confront her face-to-face.

"Adulthood," he sighs.

TRACY IS AT THE top of the curving stairwell, tying a large, furry spider to the banister with fishing wire. None of the other workers moving back and forth with paint cans and tool belts to perform fixes and add last-minute details acknowledge David as he stands in the atrium under the mother spider.

He doesn't know if he should walk up there or shout and is saved from the decision when she notices him staring up at her. She bows her head in thought, then sits on the top step and stares at him. He walks up the steps but is afraid of saying something stupid. Again, she saves him.

"I'm not in love with you," she says. "I need you to understand that."

The words pierce his ego. "Okay, then what has been going on?"

"You told me to meet you, set up your phone for me to track you, only to find you kissing someone else. Why did you do that?"

He did not consider the optics from Tracy's perspective. "I'm so sorry, Tracy; I wasn't thinking."

"That's the point, David. It wasn't just finding you kissing Kyra; it was the look in your eyes. You were drunk."

"It was a party," he states. "You weren't drinking?"

"I'm not..." she trails off and takes a deep breath.

"This is about Dad," he realizes, and it's his turn to be flushed.

She takes a moment before answering. "Your father didn't make great decisions when he was drinking, and I don't want the same thing happening to you."

"I'm not my father, Tracy."

"Neither of us knows that."

"You're not my keeper, Tracy. Not my father, my mother, or my girlfriend."

"I'm your friend," Tracy says. "Your father is gone, your mother is working her ass off, and your girlfriend hardly knows you. Dougie is going through his own shit that he won't share with either of us, and no one cares about what I want..." Her eyes well with tears.

"I care about you, Tracy. You're the only one..." he realizes what he is about to say. "Oh," his eyes widen. "Yeah, you're right. You're the only one."

Silence between them, but also understanding.

"How can I be better for you?" he asks.

She stays silent for a minute, but her face shows that she is thinking about the question.

"Be honest with me. If you want me to keep an eye on your drinking, let me. If you tell me you don't have time for a relationship, don't let me find you sitting in the dark, drunk with a stranger. Let's be the one element in each other's life that isn't an x-factor."

"I hear you, and I'm going to try to be more honest. I don't think I'm in a place for a relationship, but I do like Kyra. Seeing her there caught me off guard, and I was drunk. I'm sorry."

Her voice drops to a whisper. "Did you sleep with her last night?"

"If I did, am I the type of person to share that?"

"You'd tell me," she says.

"I would have, yes, but now that I know it might hurt your feelings..."

"I can get over it," Tracy returns her eyes toward him. "I'd rather be the person you come to for help than to have you feel like you're alone."

"Why?" he asks and then feels comfortable enough to sit next to her on the stairs.

"Why, what?"

"Why do you care about me? I mean, really. Why invest time in me? What do I bring to your table, anyone's table, that they seem to want to invest time and attention in me?"

Tracy looks over the atrium as she thinks. David realizes he might have asked a question she had never considered and just brought to light a harsh truth.

"It's what you don't bring to the table."

"What do you mean?"

"A tragedy happened to your family, and your first instinct is to place your life on hold to ensure your mother and brother are okay. You are afraid of how you will react to drinking, knowing what your father went through, so you were honest about keeping yourself in check. You're not the type of person who will sleep with someone and brag about it, and when your friend is hurting, you will swallow your pride and confront her face-to-face to heal the wound."

"That's really sweet, thank you," David says, inundated with joy. "I needed to hear that."

"Shut up," Tracy scowls. He laughs.

"To be honest, I came here to smooth things over and ask for a favor."

"Oh, really?"

"Can you take Ethan on the hayride tonight?"

"That's an awesome idea. He'll have a blast. I'm in."

"Thanks."

Tracy places an arm around his shoulders and hugs him close.

"I'm sorry about everything," he says.

"I'm going to be honest with you. I'm a little jealous of Kyra. I don't think she sees you as another conquest. I think she actually sees you the way I do, and it makes me feel less special."

"I'm sorry, I just never felt that way about you before, so when we kissed the other night... I still don't know how I feel about it."

"What do you mean?"

"I... I loved it, and I haven't stopped thinking about you as more than a friend ever since. But I don't want to make a decision based on my reaction to something new, you know?"

"I get it, and I think the idea of you possibly leaving the state for college made me react a little funky, too. Then, when everything happened with your dad, the thought of you having to stay made me just as scared. Let's take it one day at a time. Until then, let's remain a team."

He rests his head on her shoulder for a moment, then stands. "I need to do another round of checking and give Mom a call. See you at sundown?"

"Definitely."

He leaves the house and checks the time. Ethan doesn't go to school until nine, and it's only eight. He dials his mother on his way to the communications house so he can drop his clothes, the blueprint, and Dougie's phone in his laptop bag.

"David," she sighs into the phone. "Are you okay? Where have you been?"

"I'm fine," he makes himself say softly. "I was with the team last night. Sorry to make you worry. Can you put Ethan on for me?"

"Sure," she says with curiosity. He hears her tell Ethan that his brother is on the phone.

"David?" his brother answers. "Where are you?"

"Hey buddy, I have a question."

"What?" his brother bites, clearly upset with his older brother's absence. David can't wait to hear the difference in his little brother's voice after he asks him the question.

"Would you like to do something awesome tonight?"

Chapter 10

A DUST CLOUD TRAILS the horizon on the other side of the harvested cornfield. The road circumvents the grounds and then turns onto the main driveway a mile out, so even though David can see the car, it still has another five minutes before it arrives. He does not recognize the car but figures it's owned by whoever has been giving his mother a ride to and from work.

She said she is more than happy to let Ethan participate in the final dress rehearsal, which means not having to pay her night's tips to the neighbor's kid to babysit. David noticed the relief in her voice and knew it had nothing to do with money. He tucks in his attraction-themed shirt without realizing he is doing it and ensures his shoes are tied.

He runs his hand through his hair to fluff up his curls and stands at attention until the car pulls into the packed-dirt area that will serve as the parking lot for the remainder of the weekend. The car stops, and when the dust settles, he sees Oliver, the diner's cook, give him a half-hearted wave from the driver's seat.

David clenches his teeth and fights back the onset of anger at seeing his mother with another man. Surely, he is just offering a ride to and from the diner. He better be just offering a ride.

His mother exits the passenger-side door and opens the back door for Ethan. The little kid's eyes light up as he rounds the car and runs up to David like he wants to wrap his arms around him in a big hug, but then thinks better of it. David's chest tightens, knowing he has been so distant from his brother that it would make him feel this way. His mother's disappointment is apparent as well, so he kneels and wraps his arms around Ethan.

"You're going to have a blast tonight," David says. Ethan smiles and nods.

"He's excited to spend time with you, but..." his mother trails off. David knows she is considering taking him home and skipping the night shift. "He's nervous."

"What if I told you that I will be with you the whole time?"

Ethan lifts his head to look his brother in the eyes. "Really?"

David offers his hand. "Let me show you."

Ethan nods excitedly and takes his brother's hand. David stands and smiles at his mother.

"If he can't handle it, I can pick him up on the way home but—" She opens her mouth to say something else but then shakes her head.

"What?" David says.

"I just," she stammers, "You've been... different."

David wants to lash out, but that would be childish. He has been different. Different situations and people are happening to him which he doesn't know how to handle. Everyone sees him better than he sees himself, so to navigate, he might need to rely on everyone else's directions.

"Mom," David says curtly. His mother winces in preparation for an argument. "I promise you that tonight I'm getting my job done and taking care of my little brother. Those are the only things I care about."

His mother takes a deep breath and lets it out, her eyes welling up with tears. "That makes me feel a lot better, thank you." She leans in and kisses him on the cheek.

"I'm sorry," she says.

"I don't mind," he laughs.

"No, I mean—"

"I know what you meant. It's okay. Let's talk later."

She blows him a kiss and then walks back to the car. David nods at Oliver with a steeled jaw and dagger eyes, giving the older man promises that he intends to keep.

"THIS IS SO COOL. It's like making a movie!" Ethan clicks the camera switch button, sending each feed to fill the main monitor one after the other. "You made this?"

"I had help, but yeah, I can make this all on my own."

"How did you learn this?"

"I've liked making movies since Dad bought me a camera years ago."

Ethan loses his smile and hardens his concentration on the big screen. David sits in the chair next to him. "Do you want to talk about Dad, Ethan?"

Ethan stops pressing the button and puts his hands in his lap. He shakes his head slowly and looks downward.

"When you want to, just let me know, okay?" David is not sure if he wants to breach the subject either, but the urge to comfort his brother is suddenly greater than his own need to bury his sadness. "I'll be watching you from the monitors the whole time. There will be a lot of scary stuff, but remember what I told you?"

"These are your friends in masks," Ethan nods and smiles.

"That's right, they are just playing pretend," David assures him with a smile, but he can't help but think it's a lie.

The front door squeaks.

"But you might know one or two of the real monsters..."

Ethan's eyes widen. "Tracy?"

"And Dougie," although he doesn't know if that's true.

"But Tracy will be there?"

"Anyone in here ready for a spooky hayride?"

Ethan hops off the chair and runs toward Tracy. She kneels and opens her arms, but Ethan stops in the middle of the room, turns around, and races back to wrap his arms around his brother. David embraces him, and his brother's love fills him with relief. Ethan runs toward Tracy and hugs her. She looks up at David, offering him the type of smile one offers at a funeral. He mirrors the same, and mouths, *"Thank you."*

"Let's go get some ghouls," she says.

"Yeah!" Ethan shouts. She takes Ethan's hand, and they leave.

David switches the feeds on the board so he can trace their journey across the fairground toward the west, where a line of volunteers, park workers who won't get to ride tomorrow night, as well as their family and friends, wait for the hayride. Mitchell unlatches the back and waits for everyone to cram inside before closing it.

Tracy sits in the back left and pats the seat next to her. Ethan looks around and says something to her, to which she nods. She opens her legs, and Ethan sits between them. She wraps her arms around him. The trailer pitches forward. Ethan's eyes widen, and his gaze lowers towards the trailer's floor. Tracy hugs him close and says something to him that cheers him up.

She points up towards the camera that hangs off the hayride's jagged-lettered "Enter" sign. Ethan waves, and despite not being able to see him, David waves back. He texts *'Wave'* to Tracy, and on the camera, he sees her show Ethan, whose eyes light up with joy.

David watches his brother go through the ride with the mindset that he is watching a horror movie where he has a stake in the main character, a new way to absorb his favorite medium. As he imagined, Ethan did not react well to the pumpkin jumping out of the outhouse. Tracy wrapped her arms around him and hid his eyes. David saw her use the "cut throat" signal towards Mark to let him know to concentrate on someone else and is surprised he complied, considering how much ire he had shown towards David.

To David's surprise, Ethan is enamored with the Bug House. No fear of creepy crawlies, and like David, he is most likely trying to figure out "how they did it." That will be a fun conversation they can have later. The fire inside the Burn Barn captures his attention, but the higher the flames rise, the harder he digs his face into Tracy's shoulder. Ethan finds such interest in the Mad Scientist's Lab that he leans against the trailer's side and takes in the scenery... until Pam and Kevin pull off their sheets and the tables tip forward.

The two pumpkins run at top speed towards the trailer, forcing Ethan to fly back against the other side and bury his face in his arms. Tracy tries to scoot over to him, but one of the masked performers jumps into the trailer and blocks her way. Tracy tugs on Pam or Ryan's robe, but whoever it is doesn't seem to be listening. The pumpkin wraps its arms around Ethan and lifts him into the air.

David slides to the edge of his chair. He holds up his phone and hits the speed dial for Tracy without taking his eyes from the screen. The pumpkin holding Ethan lifts its feet over the trailer's side and jumps off. Ethan holds out his arms to Tracy as he is carried between the tables and towards the back of the room. Tracy jumps over the side in pursuit. The riders are either laughing or shocked, thinking that what is happening is part of the show.

The other pumpkin turns to see what everyone is staring at, seeming as though they haven't been informed about what's happening. He assumes it's Pam because Ryan is the only one of the two who has a reason to mess with him. Tracy doesn't answer her cell, so he runs out of the communications shed and heads north, through the fairgrounds. He doesn't know what is going on, but if Ryan or Mark or Kevin or whoever is trying to mess with him by terrifying his little brother, they are in for a world of hurt.

His pocket vibrates as he reaches the crops. He checks it as he runs, hoping it's a reply from Tracy, but is surprised to see Dougie's name. Although relieved to hear from his friend, he is too worried about Ethan to read the text. Then he remembers that Dougie's phone should be in his bag in the room he just left. He opens the text as he bats away stalks and sees a picture of his brother looking at the camera. A brown robe stands behind him, reaching out with the phone to take the macabre picture.

Someone who knew Dougie dropped his phone. Someone who knew David had picked it up. Someone who knew he was going to Dougie's house that night. This isn't a prank; it's a warning. The only way this could end positively is if it's Dougie himself who set this up, and even then, David doesn't know how he will react.

He leaves the corn and bounds through the forest until he hits the trail on the right side of the Burn Barn. He runs east until he reaches the open doors of the Mad Scientist's Lab. The trailer is long gone, and as he approaches the entrance, he sees neither Pam nor Ryan. The white spotlights still illuminate the table and make the white sheets glow, and the Jacob's Ladder pillars that bookend them are still throwing electricity. Someone turned these back on for dramatic flair. The audacity infuriates him. He opens his favorites app and hits Dougie's name.

He did the mash... A thrash metal version of Monster Mash screeches from the loft above.

"Ethan," he yells, and then runs under the loft and climbs the ladder. He doesn't bother being cautious by looking first before pulling into the loft.

"Surprise," his brother yells as the music cuts off. The pumpkin-masked person stands behind him, one hand on his shoulder. "They wanted to play a prank on you."

"They sure got me," David says, staring at the dripping black eyes.

"Don't be a poor sport," Ethan says, reading his brother's timidness and channeling his mother's words.

"No, it was funny, but it's getting late. We should get you home." He reaches out his hand. The hand that is draped over Ethan's shoulder flips over the cell phone, its screen still illuminated from David's unanswered call, showing the illustrated man. The other hand lifts a hunting knife and moves the blade towards where the mask's lips would be, or the lips of the person underneath, to simulate a shushing gesture. David feels a chill of fear climb up his spine.

"Let's go, Ethan," he motions, his tone as flat and serious as he can make it. The pumpkin returns the knife into the robe's pocket and pushes Ethan forward.

"Bye," Ethan waves, and then climbs down the ladder. David doesn't take his eyes off the other until his brother is on the ground. The urge to throw his body forward and shove the asshole off the loft rises, and the other must sense it because they place their hand in his pocket to get ready to use the knife. David kneels and takes the ladder while keeping the masked person in sight until he is on the ground floor. He grabs Ethan's hand and drags him out of the lab.

"You're hurting me," Ethan says.

"We need to get home," David answers. He throws a look over his shoulder to make sure the person in the mask hasn't changed their mind. He turns his attention back to the trail and sees a figure step out of the woods.

"Oh, good, you have him," Tracy says, walking closer.

"Where were you?" David shouts.

"I went after Ethan."

"He never left the lab," his voice rises. She furrows her brow and takes a step back.

"I saw them go out the side. They must have doubled back."

"Were you in on this?"

"Excuse me?"

"You scare the shit out of my brother just to get to me?"

"David?" Ethan asks, realizing his brother's anger.

"I would never do anything to hurt him," her surprise changes to match his anger, "especially not for you."

"Then why am I being threatened?"

"Threatened?"

"Are you a part of this?"

"David, I promise I have no idea..."

"Come on," he says and pulls Ethan towards the crops.

"I don't want to go in there."

"It's quicker," he says, and pulls him into the stalks.

He hears Tracy call his name, but he keeps walking. He doesn't want to believe she knows about any of this, but he is too angry, too scared, to think clearly. His biggest responsibility is to protect his family, and he needs to get his brother away from the farm.

Whatever is happening, whoever is planning it, made a mistake tonight. Taking his brother and threatening him proves that the suspicious occurrences have not just been his imagination, confusion, or a lack of experience. Gabe was threatened for knowing about something that will happen on Friday, and then he disappeared.

Elise never showed up to work, except for her shoe, which was retrieved, and her phone, which was piled alongside a costume and a garden tool caked in what looked like blood. Dougie has disappeared, and someone didn't want David to drop off his phone and confirm that his friend had disappeared against his will. The threat is real. Something is going to happen on Halloween night.

"David, you're scaring me," his brother cries.

Scared? You don't know the meaning of the word, kid. For the first time since he was a child, the farm is causing him genuine fear. And he is terrified.

Chapter 11

Friday, October 31st

Erin, the barista, places two nameless coffee cups on the counter without saying, "Good morning," and then turns to prepare another customer's order. David is dumbfounded at the change in demeanor, which the manager standing at the drive-through window notices.

The man looks from him to Erin, and then back at David. The look on his face tells David everything he needs to know about the lack of their typical friendly exchange. Erin has discovered his father's sins.

The green sign and pink morning are a blur on the periphery of his tunnel vision, and if anyone says good morning to him, he doesn't hear it. He had been hoping to seclude himself in the communications room during the workday to avoid the confrontation his ego yearns for, but was awakened by a text from John requesting his presence at the morning meeting. He will be in a room with someone who placed their hands on his brother and threatened his life.

The senior staff is spread out across the living room. John stands in the middle of the room at the entrance to the kitchen while Lillian leans on the kitchen counter behind him, pouring a cup of coffee. Kevin and Ryan are on the couch to the left, and Mark and Pam are in lounge chairs on the right. Tracy leans against the left wall behind the couch, pretending not to notice David's arrival.

The others give him a glance without a greeting, adding fuel to the fire raging inside him. One of them stole Dougie's phone and then used his brother as a threat to remain silent, most likely about Dougie's disappearance.

"As you all know, this is my last year," John says, "and it has been a pleasure to—"

"We're not all here," David's anger erupts out of his mouth. John stops talking, and all heads turn towards him.

"What do you mean?" John asks.

"Elise, Gabe, and Dougie. They're not here."

John looks down at the others. Some express confusion; others express humor. He looks back up at David. "They resigned."

"Is that what you're going with?" David asks.

"David?" John says, his annoyance showing.

"Elise never showed up for work. Her boyfriend didn't say goodbye after I heard him arguing with someone. Dougie hasn't been seen in two days, and the night that I was going to drop his phone off at his house, someone took it out of my bag and then held a knife over my brother to ensure I don't say something."

Ryan snorts and looks at Kevin.

"You think this is funny, Ryan?" David asks. "Didn't you threaten to throw me off the barn loft a few days ago?"

"I think you should go take a breath of fresh air," John says.

"I think you need to wake up, John. Something is happening here that I don't want any part of, and someone here, if not all of you, is in on it."

"David," Tracy says as she moves from the wall closer to him, "you need to calm down."

"Don't think I'm not including you in on this," he says.

"Excuse me?"

"I just told you our closest friend is missing and someone threatened me to keep it a secret, and you're telling me to calm down."

"I think you're just stressed."

"Then where is he, Tracy?" David shouts. "Should I go to his house right now? Prove it to you? The last time I suggested that in this house, Ethan was threatened."

"It was just a prank," Tracy sighs.

"Okay, it was a prank. Who did it? Confess. If it was just a prank, stand up and take a bow."

"Fine," Mark says, and stands. "It was me."

"Mark?" Kevin asks.

Lillian walks into the room and leans on the frame, arms crossed, but not angry. Contemplative. Each person looks towards each other, and then at David.

"You took my brother?"

Mark rolls his eyes and reaches into his pocket. He pulls out a cell phone and tosses it to David. "Yeah, we were hazing you because we thought you'd be cool."

David looks at the blue cover and turns on the phone. The face shows the anime wallpaper. "Where is Dougie?"

"I was going to ask you. I went through your bag while you were waiting for your brother to get here so I could find something embarrassing. I found that instead. Had I known the guy was actually missing, I would have thought better of it."

David stares at the phone, dizzy with confusion. "No," he says, "I don't buy it. Why isn't he here?"

"I don't know," Mark says, "but he hasn't shown up or called in, and you have his phone. Out of all of us, you're the only one here with a history of violence. Maybe you got drunk and followed in daddy's footsteps."

"Fuck you," David runs at Mark and grabs his shirt. He lifts his other hand and is about to beat the other man in the head with Dougie's phone until Tracy steps between them. He hesitates just enough to release Mark's shirt.

John steps forward. "I'm no longer asking you, I'm telling you, as your employer, go to my office and wait for me."

David looks at him for a moment, and then around at the other faces. Everyone is dead-eyed staring at him, and the tension in the air tightens. David walks forward and bumps Mark as he passes, then stomps up the stairway. He opens the office door and moves across the room to the window behind John's desk. He places his forehead against the cold glass and tries to will his anger to subside. His phone vibrates, and when he pulls it out, he sees a text from Kyra: *Just got a text from Kevin, says you're freaking out. What's going on?*

He thumbs his phone to reply but sees that his battery is only at eight percent. He was so stressed and tired when he brought Ethan home last night, he passed out without plugging it in. He sits at John's desk and opens drawers, looking for a charger. He rummages through drafting paper, pastel chalk, and wood scraps but finds nothing except for two D batteries and a silver remote with two large buttons. The frustration keeps his anger high. He sits back in the chair and replies to Kyra: *Meet me at my station in ten.*

He stares at the door, waiting for John to enter, and notices a distinct design on one of the sketches on the wall. The head of a snake, exactly like Kyra's tattoo. He stands and walks over to the wall, lifting the evil teddy bear sketch pinned on top to reveal a pencil drawing of Kyra with a large bust of Medusa covering her back. She is kneeling on the floor and holding her hair up as she looks back at the artist. Her body is completely nude.

His anger, his fear, his jealousy; it all coalesces into an unprecedented feeling that tells him if John enters the room, he will destroy any potential for a partnership the other man has offered. Part of him is okay with that. He rips the picture from the pin and folds it into his pocket, then walks down the steps without hurry or emotion, an act of defiance. The others watch him cut through the group and exit the house without saying a word.

DAVID RETURNS TO THE shed to grab his backpack before leaving. He turns to walk out when he is startled by a figure standing at the entrance wearing the same drippy-eyed pumpkin mask and robe that the entire staff will wear that night. The wearer's hand reaches inside the robe and pulls out a silver fishhook and then lifts it in a threatening manner. David drops his bag and runs to the back of the room, grabs a box cutter from the equipment shelf, and thumbs the button to extend the blade.

"Woah," a muffled voice yells from behind the mask. The pumpkin throws the hook down and lifts the mask over their head. Kyra's long hair cascades down her worried face. "I was just trying to cheer you up. You know... Halloween... yay?"

David sighs and slams the box cutter onto the shelf. "I'm leaving."

"What's going on?"

"I keep asking myself the same question when what I should be asking is, 'Why does no one else see what's going on?'"

Kyra sets the large pumpkin head on the desk and says, "What are you talking about?"

David pulls out the nude sketch, unfolds it, and then drops it on the floor between them. Kyra stares at it for a few seconds and looks back up at him.

"What's your point?"

"I don't know whether this has become some kind of cult, or if you've become jaded to everything fucked up going on here, but something is going on here."

"What do you think is going on, David?"

"Three people are missing. My brother and I were threatened. The only reason I can find that connects these things is that I overheard something is going to happen tonight that no one can know about."

"You're talking about a conspiracy," Kyra says, thinking through his words. "Are you implying that the others were... what... murdered?"

He knows it sounds ridiculous, yet he can't unclench his stomach.

"Please, Kyra, talk me out of it. Tell me that I'm stressed, or angry, or something."

"Where's your proof?" she asks without expressing an emotion that might clue him into knowing if she believes him.

"My word isn't good enough?" he says.

"Given your family's history, your word isn't much to go on."

The words sting his heart, and his already emotionally burdened mind cracks.

"Fuck you," he says. "Or were you just trying to distract me? Were you the one who took Ethan last night? Did John tell you to do it? Ryan? Mark? What are you planning?"

She remains emotionless, unblinking, unmoving, until tears well in her eyes.

"I thought you were different, David." She turns to leave, but then stops and looks back. "You need to talk to someone, David, because I don't know you, and you obviously don't know me. Let's keep it that way. Just professional." She leaves the room. Her footsteps announce her growing distance as she leaves the building.

Just professional? Fine. This should just be professional. Whether or not he is right that something sinister is happening at the farm, he is not going to be able to think it through without divorcing himself from the situation. The more he tries to connect with these people, the more he risks becoming blinded to what is going on.

Kyra is correct; he does need to talk to someone. Someone who is far away from this situation. Someone who has been in the deep end of a disastrous professional situation. Someone who has been through childhood and adulthood, who can guide him through this nebulous world of trust and mistrust, innocence and guilt. David needs to talk to his father.

Chapter 12

THE BITTER COLD OF winter has yet to settle, so the trees retain their vibrancy of reds, yellows, and oranges. David daydreams of costumes, peanut butter cups, and horror movie marathons as he ascends the hills of the New Jersey and Pennsylvania border, trying to relax his shaking body and keep himself from turning towards the guardrail and letting gravity take his life instead of whatever hell he is currently descending into.

The scenic descent releases him into a paler view of dried-out, flat farmland. His destination is a black spot on the western horizon, a stain in the middle of an otherwise pink sky, growing bigger and more ominous as the miles close the distance. David had to call ahead to schedule the meeting, so as he pulls up to the iron gate, a suited man in a pumpkin tie and a police officer await his arrival. The man approaches and leans down to the window as David lowers the glass.

"Happy Halloween, Mr. Earhart. Pull around to the left and park. Officer Paulson will escort you inside." Before David can thank him, he jogs into a security booth, and a moment later, the gate opens. David rounds the building and parks. The officer waits for him in front of a door, unlocks it, and escorts him through two more locked doors, a metal detector, a gate, and another locked door, where he steps aside to let David enter.

David's father sits alone in a room full of unoccupied tables, standing when he sees David enter. Concentrating on superficial details helps David cross the room. His father's hair is shorter, his face is skinnier, and a green onesie makes him look younger. The last time he saw him has been burned into his mind's eye, hunched over a courtroom table, eyes sunken and far away, hands shaking. The verdict had just been read. Five years for negligent manslaughter.

Lucas Earhart was a foreman for Cohan Construction, a century-old New Jersey business. He emailed his project leader, Eric Ives, about buying a new shelving system for their next project after noticing the support columns for theirs had been damaged in transit. Eric replied that if they waited for the manufacturer to send a new unit, they would be behind schedule. The negligence caused a collapse, killing Phillip Langley, one of the construction workers working under Lucas.

At least, that's what Lucas claimed. The prosecutor showed a different email from the defendant's account: "The new one came damaged, but I'll use it until you can order another." The reply from Eric Ives was a direct order not to proceed until they acquired a new one, along with an explanation of the legality of willfully ignoring damaged equipment.

Lucas insisted that when he had sent them, they were worded differently and must have been doctored, even when it was argued that he must have sent them while he was drinking on the job. David wanted to believe his father was innocent, but the emails, along with his history of drinking, made the lawyer's argument convincing.

David awkwardly crosses the room until his father smiles, then, every emotion he has felt in the past year pushes him to close the distance as quickly as his shaking legs will and wrap his arms around the man in a tight embrace.

"You're okay," his father says, holding his son's head against his chest as he sobs into it.

David feels the gathering uncertainty and fear in his body pour out. He wants to stop crying, but his body won't let him.

"Tell me," his father says. The concern in his voice helps David let go and look at his face. His father motions for his son to sit and repeats, "Tell me."

"I will, but," David breathes in and lets it out, "I'm sorry I haven't visited, and—"

"Don't worry about it; I get it. Tell me what's going on."

That moment of permission is all David needs to unleash every detail of the past week. When he finishes, his father remains contemplative for at least two minutes.

"Dad?"

"Two possibilities remain in front of you. Either something dangerous is happening, or they are just a group of eccentric, immature people who have been working together so long in the same environment that they don't even see how toxic their relationships are becoming."

David nods his head. His father looks away again. David is not used to his father remaining silent for so long, and wonders if his change in demeanor is due to his sobriety or to everything he has been through, including his current incarceration.

"When I look back on what went wrong," he says, "it wasn't just the choices I made that I regret, but the choices I didn't. The emails I could have printed before they were intercepted. The security footage I could have pulled during the night's deliveries before they were erased. The things that could have proven my innocence. Yes, I was drinking on the job, but nothing that happened was because of my drinking."

"Dad," David sighs. He had hoped his father's denial would have been reconciled by now.

"I know I have a problem, I don't deny that, but I also know I'm very good at my job, because I put my family first and my job keeps... kept, food on the table."

David remembers his reaction to Ethan being taken and how he treated Tracy afterwards. Even though he regrets lashing out at her, his fear for his family made him react with determination, not retraction, and that gives him a small amount of pride within the pain.

"The accident wasn't my fault, but the drinking made me blind to everyone around me. There were other signs that corners were being cut by management. Had I the wherewithal..." he looks away for a moment and then back at David, "If I were sober, I would have been able to see more."

David realizes what his father is implying. His mother must have told his father.

"I've only been drinking at parties, not while working."

"Oh, we will be talking about that, David, but that's not what I'm getting at. What I'm saying is that you owe it to yourself and your family to protect yourself and trust your instincts. I once gave you the advice to keep your head down and get a paycheck, but I was wrong. You need to keep your head up and look at the details."

Details. David considers the situation at the farm. Lillian's homestead is nearly dead, so she wouldn't do anything to compromise the one attraction that keeps it afloat. John is leaving for more money, so he has no reason to sabotage the attraction he built. Mark and Ryan are assholes, but he can't see any reason why they would want to do anything to harm their friends or the farm. Kyra benefits from running the place next year. He hardly knows Kevin or Pam.

Perhaps the thing "happening on Friday night" isn't sinister at all? But if it isn't, why did three people disappear? Then again, maybe Elise and Gabe did resign? Maybe Dougie is avoiding coming to work because of whatever is going on with him? Maybe Mark had been hazing him?

"What if it's all in my head?"

The guard who led David in walks up to the table. At first, David thinks his time with his father is over, and his heart sinks. Then, the guard drops two king-sized Reese's.

"Happy Halloween, Luke and son," the guard says and then walks back towards his post at the door to the holding cells.

"Thanks, Connor," his father replies.

David looks at the chocolate in front of him and can't reconcile what he has heard about prison and the nicety on the table. His father must have read the look on his face.

"It's a minimum security prison, David." His father opens the cup in front of him. He pulls apart his plastic as well.

"I was wondering why you haven't Shawshank'd your way out of here already."

"To be honest..." His father takes a bite of the cup and places it down, his mood melting into a somber state.

"Tell me," David says.

His father closes his eyes, takes a deep breath, and exhales slowly, an action David has never seen him perform.

"I'm innocent, David. Completely. It kills me that there is any doubt of that in you, but—"

"Dad, I—"

"Let me just get this out." He waits for David's response, and when his son nods with approval, he continues. "Every day without my family is an absolute punishment for every sin I've ever committed, willingly or not, and I know the toll it has taken on you, on the family. That being said, I've been sober for over a year, have a support group and a therapist who is teaching me how to be mentally healthy. I know that's selfish, but it's honest, and I've been told that honesty is the key to a healthy life for me and for you."

David takes a bite of his cup to fill his mouth with anything other than words he might say without thinking. If his father is innocent of what brought him here, then life is cruel. However, if he is innocent and still can utilize the cruelty to heal from other forms of suffering, then...

"Life is difficult and weird," is all David can surmise about his family's current status. He wishes he had more complicated words or more insight, but somehow that childish statement feels equally appropriate for this adult situation.

"Life is fucking difficult and weird," his father agrees. "And so are the people in it."

People. The word brings back the face and the myriads of personalities he's had to navigate. Strangers with secrets. Close friends with secrets. Distrustful relationships. Tenuous partnerships. His introduction to the adult world is disheartening at best and terrifying at worst.

"Can I be honest with you, too?" David asks.

"Of course."

"It feels better to believe you are guilty."

His father eats the remaining piece of his cup and sits back in his chair.

"I don't believe you intended to hurt anyone, obviously, but I imagine what your reasoning would be if you did use the damaged equipment on purpose. You would do it to ensure the project finished on time, which means you would get paid on time. You'd do it because that meant your family wasn't wanting for anything we would need. Even if you were drinking at the time and didn't think it through, I could understand that. Both of those reasons make me angry, but I can see how they could happen. But someone lying about a death? Faking emails to frame an innocent man? I can't get over what that says about people..." He trails off because he feels like he is going to break. His father leans forward and places his arms on the table.

"I'm not going to lie to you, David. People are capable of making terrible decisions. You just laid out the reasoning for it. The lengths I would go to for my family... It's unimaginable. I don't forgive Ives for what he did, but he also had a project to finish, a family to consider. He has a son going to Yale and a wife who has a brain tumor the size of a grapefruit. The future of his family relies on where their money comes from and where it's allocated. That's an impossible situation, and in that situation, I might be okay with framing an innocent man to ensure my family has the best chance at life."

David can't help but cry at his father's words, not just because they are hard to hear, but because he understands the harsh truth behind them.

"How do I move through a world where I can't trust anyone?"

"I never said you can't trust anyone, David, just that there are people in desperate situations."

"How can I tell the difference?"

"That's a good question," his father says, sitting back in his chair, looking away. After a few seconds, he leans forward again. "Motivation. Think of it like you are watching a mystery movie.

Who gains from whatever is happening? Who loses something, or is about to lose something?"

David thinks back to all the iconic antagonists in cinema history, but most of them had no real motive other than killing. Freddy Kruger is addicted to killing children. Hannibal Lecter is a cannibal. Michael Myers is just evil... depending on which remake. Their lack of motive terrified him as a child because he couldn't imagine someone who enjoys making others suffer.

"What if it's just some maniac who wants to see people suffer?"

"I said mystery, not horror. Real life is less sensational. You said you heard a guy's voice saying that something is being planned. Unless you are dealing with a serial killer who likes to kill for fun, there's a motive and a reason behind it, however convoluted or ill-informed. No one plans to disappear people without a compelling reason, or a way to get away with it if they are successful. Horror movie villains never plan for what happens if they get away with it. Real-life people know they aren't going to be able to hide behind the end credits."

"So you believe me?" David asks, and then realizes he doesn't want the answer.

"Honestly? I don't know, it all seems too happenstance, but that's my point. No one believed that my boss found a way to hack computers and fake emails, but that's what happened. The question is, what if I didn't believe you and something awful happened? What if you are in danger? I'm not taking the chance of doing nothing and letting my family suffer. Not again. Besides, you have it worse than I did. You'd be surprised what people think they can get away with if they're hiding behind a mask. That's one thing horror movies get right. So, if you did not doubt that this is all happening, that people have been threatened and are missing, and something worse is about to happen, then what can we do to prove it?"

David feels relief at his father's use of "We," and understands that his father's inflection is not asking what they can do as a means to brainstorm, but to prompt David into realizing a conclusion that his father has already made. "If I act like I'm keeping my head down, no one is looking at me."

"Exactly," his father smiles. "And you'll be alone with the video feeds all night. You're police surveillance."

"I can record everything," David thinks, and then realizes a grave detail, "but I don't think a person would risk doing something on camera."

"Then don't look where they think you're looking." His father smiles the same way he used to when trying to get David to notice a detail on screen when they watched movies.

"I have a few extra cameras I can use. Point them in places other than the attractions..." David sits back in his chair, deep in thought. "Catch the culprit going towards the crime scene instead of waiting for a crime scene to happen."

"You know what I always say about the power of filmmaking," his father says, sitting back in his chair, mimicking his son's movement.

"If it's on camera, it's real," David says.

His father leans forward. "And if it's real, you can capture it on camera."

Chapter 13

Keeping his head down is harder than David expected, since every face turns towards him with suspicion as he reenters the farm. Word of his outburst has traveled fast, and he wonders who, if not more than one person, has spread the gossip. None of the senior staff pays him attention, and although his heart aches when Kyra passes him on the hayride trail without saying a word, he is glad to move unimpeded.

The only one who doesn't care about his passing is Mitchell, smoking a cigar and sitting by the unlit bonfires, resting the hour before the gates open. David wonders if he should ask the older man for any insight about the farm but realizes it might be too late to use any details he can gather. David has a plan, and he needs to be ready before the gates open. Choosing which places to set up the cameras is more difficult than actually setting them up.

A minicam along the outer edge of the Haunted Maze, looking upwards at the Badger's house, and another pointing towards the front of the walkthrough haunted house, where he had seen someone collect Elise's shoe. He placed another along the hayride trail between the Outhouse and Bug House, and another between the Burn Barn and the Mad Scientist's Lab.

The last one he set up on the shelf in the communications room to view himself and the monitor bay, in case someone tries to threaten him or if he needs to account for his whereabouts when it, whatever it is, goes down. All the new feeds he displays on his laptop are directly from the converter box. The audience won't be able to access them because the attraction feeds are broadcast from the main monitor. His phone vibrates with a text message, and as he pulls it from his pocket, he hopes to see Dougie's name on its face. Instead, it's an unknown number.

Are you at the monitors?

Who is this? He has no time for distractions.

Can you see me?

He peruses the eight feeds on the main monitor, but none of the workers are on their phones or looking at the camera. He is about to text back until he notices movement on the bottom of the two CRTs on the right. The top of a face fills the view, its camera mounted to a post in the haunted maze. Mark's face, he thinks, until the man steps back and reveals a bare chin.

I see you. He texts Kevin.

We need to talk in private. Come here.

I don't have time for whatever you want, he replies.

I think I know what you were talking about, but I don't want to share it where it can be saved.

David's heart races, but he knows better than to follow any of the senior staff's words blindly: *How do I know this isn't another fucking joke?*

Three dots appear, disappear, and then reappear. The answer that arrives forces David out of the building and into the haunted maze.

I know where Dougie has been.

KEVIN IS LIGHTING A cigarette in the heart of the maze. David stands at the entrance and calls his name softly, not to startle him. Kevin turns around and walks close enough to almost choke David with the smoke he exhales.

"I think you're right about something going on tonight."

"Okay. What about Dougie?"

"I don't know where Dougie is."

"Dammit, Kevin," he yells.

"Keep your voice down. I mean that I don't know where he is, but I think you're right that he's in trouble."

"How do you know?"

Kevin takes another drag and exhales the smoke. He averts his eyes as he says, "I'm the one he was meeting the night of the party."

David takes a moment to process the information and its implications.

"He was supposed to meet me at my apartment, but never showed up. He even used you as an excuse so his mother didn't expect him home that night."

"You and Dougie are friends?"

Kevin looks at him with disappointment. "David."

David remembers the text and its recipient labeled as "Crush."

"Dougie is gay?" He doesn't so much ask that of Kevin, but of himself. "I knew he was struggling with something, angry even, but..." Then he remembers Dougie talking about Pam, and her saying that she has hardly spoken with Dougie. "I think you need to talk to your friend," she had said. Had she known? Was David oblivious to his friend's troubles because of his own?

"What about your brother?" he asks. "Did he know?"

Kevin looks at the hay-filled ground again and takes another drag.

"That's what I can't understand, why my brother would lie."

"Lie about what?" David's frustration boils over.

"Last night, after he scared your brother at the Outhouse and watched over the Bug House, Mark and I walked back to Lillian's to get something to eat. He couldn't have been the one to grab your brother."

"Why would he lie about something like that?"

Kevin drops his cigarette on the ground and steps on it.

"Exactly. He would have loved to play a prank like that, or rat out anyone else who did it just for a laugh. If he felt the need to keep the person behind the mask a secret, that—"

"That means the threat is real, and he is covering for whoever was under the mask."

"Or, it was Dougie under the mask, and they are both messing with me."

"Why would Dougie mess with you if he likes you?"

"I was hoping you would tell me. Dougie and I just started getting to know each other."

"I guess I don't know him well enough," David realizes. "But I don't think he would do something this involved. Missing work? Giving up his cell for a prank? I don't think he would get involved with whatever Mark is involved in."

"But you just admitted that you're unsure." Kevin stays silent as David processes this information.

"I guess you're right. Could your brother have influenced him in some way?"

"Maybe? Look, I love my brother, David, but I also know he gets into things, risky things. I don't know what is going on, but there is a reason he had Dougie's phone and a reason he took the blame other than to amuse himself. I thought it was because he's embarrassed that I'm gay and was messing with Dougie and me to make him feel better, but getting you involved with that doesn't make sense."

"Okay, so Mark is planning something or knows someone who is planning something. What do we do?"

"I don't know, but I wanted you to know you're not alone. If my brother is into something, and it is happening tonight, keep your eyes on the cameras and let me know if you see anything."

"Kevin, I have eyes everywhere."

"Good," Kevin nods, and a slight red ring forms under his eyes.

"I'm sorry," David says. "We'll find Doug."

"I'm sorry too," he says, and then walks into the stalks.

As DAVID WALKS BACK to communications, he sees the line to get into One Fright Only stretch from the gated entrance and down the main road. Hordes of Jack-o'-lantern faces smile and sneer as they wait for their victims to enter. Theremin-laden music seeps from the main speakers around the fairground.

The rides and booths come alive, throwing colors and sounds into the night. In the distance, a tractor's engine revs. The gates open.

CHAPTER 14

LOOKING AT THE REVELRY through the monitors and the walls of his bunker helps David separate the distractions from his objective. Viewing it through his favorite medium used to be an exciting prospect, a way to make money while pretending he's a part of something he loved doing in his past, but this week has tainted so much of his experience that despair has seeped into his nostalgia. He's not just jealous that everyone else is having fun. He's resentful. He's seen behind the mask, and the face of adulthood is anything but innocent.

He watches the extra feeds on his laptop with feverish intent. A good director considers every millimeter of the screen. If he looks at what he has seen as a director and not a viewer, how does every scene before this moment dictate the ending?

Screams overtake the music from outside in short bursts from those already reveling in their victim status as they move through the fairground. Booths are packed, and the food and drinks are flowing. Passengers on the hayride are horrified at what they are looking at, their faces strobed by the light of spiders crawling up the cabin wall. A woman inside the haunted house breaks from the man she is with to run out of the room filled with mummies. Two young men make out in one of the corn maze's dead ends. Near the bonfires are three middle school-aged girls dressed like undead cheerleaders, dancing like the zombies from the Thriller music video.

A widget on the flat screen shows participation on the site has breached a thousand. The number isn't impressive by Internet standards, but it is indicative of popularity. Comments on the main page are positive:

"I can watch this all night."

"What an awesome idea!"

"Yo, that's my mom!"

"I hope they do this next year!"

He uses the mouse to click on the camera that looks down onto the Burn Barn's floor. The tractor pulls into the right side of the frame and leaves through the left, leaving the trailer and its passengers perfectly framed in view. A wave of déjà vu hits his mind and causes a dizzying sensation. Something about the colors in the image, or the arrangement of people around the trailer, reminds him of the dress rehearsal. He sees only the tops of their heads, but like the rehearsal, there is a guy with a bald spot in the top middle and a woman with pink hair in the bottom right. There's even a smaller boy with the same dirty blonde straight hair as his brother...

The dizziness of experiencing déjà vu hits him harder.

"What the hell?" He clicks the switcher several times to bring the barn's main camera full screen and then picks up the phone to call his mother. She answers on the third ring.

"Hey, honey, you okay?"

"Is Ethan with you right now?" He stares at the top of his brother's head as he pulls back from the flames that rise from the side of the trailer. Over the top of the trailer's side, he thinks he also sees Tracy's red hair, but she should be working in the haunted house.

"Yeah, we just started walking the neighborhood."

A boy's voice screams, "Trick or treat" in the distance. David hangs up and clicks the icon to display a complete view of all eight feeds. On the bottom right, the timestamp reads 10/31/2025.

"That's impossible." He places his hands on his head and crosses his fingers inside his curls. How is a video from yesterday playing when everything else is live? His eyes unfocus from the single image as he thinks, helping him notice that the coloration in the barn's feed is more washed out than the others, and grainier.

The camera could be producing a different image because of the fire's high heat, or contrasted poorly by the extreme light and dark, or a hundred other factors, but his editing experience tells him otherwise. The darker corners of the video do not change grain or gain, telling him that the footage has been compressed, as if it had been exported, and is now playing back from an external source.

But every transmitter ends in this room, he thinks. It's live, so no one can hack in and place an image on top of the feeds in the software...

He grabs the edge of the desk and pulls it at least a foot from the wall. He leans around the monitor to see the connecting hardware. Each camera receiver box is plugged into the black box, except for the one for the barn. That's lying next to it, and in its place is an HDMI cord attached to an external disc drive. The footage feeding into the black box is not live, but is playing from a disc.

He stands up to look at the monitor. The trailer drives out of the frame as the flames die. A few seconds later, the footage flickers. Nearly imperceptible, but David had an inkling it would be there. A few seconds later, a trailer drives in from the right side of the frame. As the back of the trailer moves into view, he sees Tracy and his brother sitting in the corner. David detaches the HDMI cord from the box and plugs in the camera receiver. Three green dots blink intermittently as the receiver tries to grab a signal from its transmitter on the camera.

The image that pops onto the feed is too chaotic for his brain to comprehend. Flames fully engulf the back of the trailer, the crackling sound popping through the camera's tiny microphone beside screams from people off-camera. In the bottom left corner, a teenage boy wraps his arms around a child, pulling her away as a piece of wood from the trailer's side falls off and spreads flames as it lands.

The box for opening the doors in case of an emergency lies on the floor, its battery compartment open and empty. A jacket is thrown in the middle of the fire, and a young woman jumps on top. She looks up at the camera and waves her arms. The right side of her sweater has burned off, and smoke rises from her body.

"Help," she cries. "We can't get out!"

DAVID KNOCKS INTO PATRONS as he snakes through the rides, concession stands, and game booths. "Something is wrong with the barn doors, and the failsafe is missing batteries," he calls into the walkie- talkie to the other senior staff. "Kyra, open the doors. Someone call nine-one-one!"

"David, say that again." John's voice.

He breaches the edge of the fairgrounds at the cornstalks and lifts the walkie to speak again but hesitates. Someone went out of their way to sabotage that camera so he wouldn't see what was happening. It can only be one of the senior staff, and all of them heard that message.

"It doesn't matter," he says aloud. People are in trouble. He lifts the walkie-talkie.

"The ride is trapped inside, and the fire has spread out of the fire zone. Kyra, are you there?"

Why isn't she answering?

"You better not be fucking around," Ryan says.

"David, return to your post," John says. "Kyra, come in."

David doesn't know if John thinks he's exaggerating, but he doesn't have the breath to argue and run at the same time. He nearly falls twice on downed stalks and large stones, but he makes it out in less than two minutes to see flames blazing beyond the forest's edge. The heat from the fire rises as he steps onto the trail, forcing him to stop in fear of burning. Luckily, Kyra is there, watching the flames pour out of the top of the barn.

"Open the doors!" he screams to her. Flames lick from beneath both sides of the doors, telling him that grabbing them and forcing them open isn't an option. He thinks she might be in shock, so he pivots to the right and heads for the stand holding the utility box. Kyra turns and blocks his way.

"I can't let you do that, David." She stands firm, but her eyes are full of fear.

"What do you mean? People are going to get hurt."

"Lillian already called. Firefighters are on their way. Let's wait for them."

"They might not get here in time; we need to let them out."

"They'll be fine. It's rigged to look like it's not under control, but it is."

David wants to argue, but he realizes what she is saying. This is the plan. A controlled disaster, and she has planned it.

"I'm not taking that chance," he says, letting his anger show. Not just his anger, but his disappointment. His heartbreak. He pushes her aside and tries to lift the metal cover, but it doesn't open. A key lock is on the side. He turns to see Kyra pulling the key from her pocket.

"Give me the key, Kyra."

"It's going to be okay," she says, her shoulders lowering and her eyes welling. "I'll explain it all later. You have to trust me."

"Like you said, I don't even know you."

Her tears fall then, but she shakes her head. "I can't. My entire future depends on this."

David pulls out his phone and opens the streaming app to navigate to the inside footage. The camera has fallen off the stand and shows a tilted image of the room. Flames engulf the loft's central post. Mitchell and several others are trying to break through the back wall under the loft. Fire rains down from between the wood panels above. He moves closer to Kyra and holds up the phone to show her the chaos.

"Does that look contained to you?

"I don't..." she stammers, and looks confused. "It was just supposed to be the walls..." She turns around, runs to the box, and uses its key to open the panel. She presses one of the large buttons. "What the fuck?"

"What?" David asks, even though he guesses what she is about to say. She continues to press them all, but nothing happens.

"This worked a minute ago. I don't understand..." She turns to look at him. "This wasn't the plan."

"Whose plan?" he asks, but realizes that her wide, wild eyes are not looking at him, but behind him. He turns to see a pumpkin head looking down at him. It snatches the phone out of his hands. He backs away towards the forest, but sees another pumpkin costume emerge.

"Call for help," he tells the newcomer, "They—" but realizes that the person under the mask is walking too slowly, too purposefully, for someone who is in a panic about the barn being on fire. David backs away from the three of them and down the trail towards the Lab.

His body collides with something else. He turns to see the pumpkin looming down on him, close enough that he does not see the raised fist behind its head until it is already inches away from colliding with his head.

Chapter 15

David feels pain pulsating in his head before he opens his eyes. His body slumps forward but remains aloft. He looks down and sees that he is sitting in a chair with duct tape wrapped around his chest and thighs. He looks up and is not surprised to see John's blurred face in front of him. Although the man is talking, his voice is muffled.

He looks around to survey his surroundings and to force his eyes to focus. He recognizes the layout: the cot against the wall, the desk, and the colors around the walls of John's office. Kyra's form is recognizable at the window as she stares out of it at the colorful Ferris wheel in the distance. In the back of his mind, he is processing the heartbreak of her involvement as well as John's betrayal, but he tries to think past that and figure out a way to escape.

The idea that every dream of a proper future this man promised him will never come to fruition makes him want to scream, but the prospect of no future at all takes precedence. He tenses his muscles and moves his body against the duct tape, hoping to find some give or tear he can exploit. He tries to stand, but discovers that the tape wrapped around his legs is threaded under the seat to hold him in place. John's voice sharpens, and its quality grabs his attention, realizing that John isn't talking to him or Kyra, but to someone else on the other side of the room.

"...when did you go insane?" John says, his voice straining with desperation. "What about you, Kyra? When did you all go insane?"

David realizes that John is also tied to a chair in the same fashion. Kyra folds her arms and continues to stare out of the window. The floor behind him creaks, and he feels someone standing at his side.

"I'm the one who's insane?" A woman's voice, possibly Lillian's. "You fuck children for fun, John."

"You hear that, Kyra?" John laughs. "She's calling you a child. You sure she's the one you want to throw yourself behind?"

Kyra turns around and moves towards John with her finger raised. The other person's hand lifts to stop her, sending her to lean against the wall. "You took over everything," Kyra spits with a face contorted with rage. "Groomed everyone into joining you. Manipulated everyone. Now that the money is gone, you want to leave."

"Do you even hear yourself, Kyra?" he seethes through his teeth, breathing heavily. "Grooming? Manipulating? Is that what she told you?" He nods towards the other person standing just beyond David's peripheral vision. "It's not my fault you all looked up to me. This was a job. A gig I got paid for. The job doesn't pay anymore, so I need to look for another one. Any other reason beyond what she might have told you is manipulation. It's a cult, and she's the leader."

"Shut the fuck up!" the woman screams and lunges into David's view. Lillian pulls a steak knife from her jeans' waist. She grabs John's hair with her free hand and pulls his head back to rest the blade on his neck.

"Lillian, calm down," Kyra pleads as she pushes off the wall and lifts her hands.

"Calm down?" She cackles. "He doesn't care about us. We are supposed to be a family."

David sees John wince, then notices a line of red form where the blade is pressing. If she doesn't pull away, her anger might cut him too deeply. But what can he say that will distract her? He hardly knows her, and if he wants to get help, the only person he can count on is Kyra. If she is as surprised about the knife as he is, she might not want this to go too far.

"Wasn't Elise part of your family?"

Lillian turns her head and stares daggers at him, then lets go of John to turn the knife on him. He doesn't know whether to be relieved or terrified.

"I loved Elise," Lillian cries. The look on Kyra's face reveals that this is news to her as well.

"Then where is she?" David asks. "What about Gabe? Did you kill him, too?"

Lillian takes a step closer, her face full of anger and another emotion he can't identify.

"She didn't kill anybody," Kyra sighs. "She paid them off."

David wants desperately to believe that, and is somewhat relieved that's what Kyra thinks, but the look in Lillian's eyes as they shift towards Kyra tells a darker story. He wants to accuse her again, keep her talking, but that might further enrage her. Even though he feels bad for the others, there is a personal mystery that needs to be answered.

"Was Dougie 'paid off'? If I went to his house right now, would he be there?" The emotion on Lillian's face drains away, leaving a lifeless stare.

"Lillian?" Kyra asks as she steps away from the wall.

"What was the plan, Lil?" questions John, his voice nearly a whisper. "Sue me for negligence?"

"That was exactly..." Kyra says with astonishment.

"How, Kyra? Shit, I'm the one who bought the fire insurance."

"That's not what it will look like to the cops," Lillian says with a hint of a smile.

"What?"

"It's amazing what hackers can do these days. You think you're so fucking smart, John." She waves the knife towards John again.

"No," he scowls, "just smarter than you. I've been keeping your farm alive for years since you were too stupid to do it. Your parents had no problem with it. Hell, Mitchell could have kept it going, but you had to take control. That's what it's all about, isn't it? Control. You don't think of any of them as family. Me,

Kyra, or any of the others. It's because your real family is gone, and you fucked up everything they left you."

David wants to scream at John not to antagonize her further, but the man's eyes keep shifting between Lillian and Kyra, telling David that he has come to the same conclusion. Kyra does not know the extent of what she has gotten into, and if she did, she might act in their favor.

"I'm going to kill you," Lillian says without a hint of emotion. Her seriousness grabs John's attention, and he stays quiet as the blade's tip points directly at his neck. "And I'm going to blame you for a lot of harm. You will become the boogeyman you always wanted to be."

"Lillian, it's done," Kyra says. "The fire department and ambulances are already arriving. You changed the emails, I planted the batteries, Pam gave me pictures of him practically beating her, and the others did their part. David won't say a word once we tell him how much money we can get from John's streaming deal. No one will believe him over us. Let him go."

But Lillian isn't listening. She is locked in a staring contest with John, and the tip of her blade draws closer to his Adam's apple.

"She killed them, Kyra," David cries. "Just like she's letting everyone in the barn burn. That's why she sabotaged my camera and the door switch to ensure help wouldn't arrive in time. Having victims means someone will need to take the fall."

"Tell me that's not true," she demands as she steps closer to David's chair. "They were family."

"I gave them a chance to be family," Lillian says. "To keep alive a farm that has served this land since the turn of the century. It survived droughts, deluges, and economic depression. They didn't want to fight for it, so they don't get to claim they're *family*. They're employees who didn't measure up."

Kyra places a hand over her mouth. Her face pales. She places her other hand on the back of David's chair and leans forward as though she is about to throw up. Her eyes search for a meaning or a reason that they can't find.

"Don't leave me now, Kyra. We've come too far."

She shakes her head. "I know. I know you're right."

"Kyra," David says, desperate to have her stay sane. "Dougie was my friend. He didn't deserve any of this."

Lillian laughs. "Your friend betrayed you, David."

David looks at her, his stomach clenching. "What do you mean?"

"Lillian, don't," Kyra pleads.

"Who do you think kept tabs on you and Gabe? He told Kyra everything, even the backup program you had on your laptop." Lillian glares at him, and something in her expression tells him that she carries at least a modicum of sympathy.

David's heart breaks, and his already twisted stomach feels like it is going to pull apart. Dougie's warning the night of the party about getting involved with the group. He thought the others might be involved, but not Dougie.

"It doesn't matter," Kyra shakes her head. "She's right. We've come too far, and this is for the greater good of the farm and all of us." She looks at David. "You too, if you're with us." She takes her hand off the back of the chair and places it on his back. "With me."

David looks in her eyes and offers only disappointment. Her hand rubs his back, but instead of arousal, he is disgusted.

"You were just using me," he laments, "just like you are now."

"No," she demands. "Nothing I said about my feelings for you was a lie." Her eyes plead with him to hear her words, to pay attention, and he realizes that the movement on his back is too mechanical to be seductive. She's using her pocketknife to split the tape.

"You told me you love me?" he states plainly, not trusting his acting skills to sell his vulnerability.

"I do love you. I'm in love with you." She nods, steely-eyed, selling her conviction, making him believe that she is serious.

Despite the unique desperation of his predicament, he feels something for her that he desperately wants to be true. She leans forward and kisses him. He pretends to hesitate at first, but then pushes back, kissing her with more passion than he has kissed anyone. She leans closer so that their bodies are nearly touching, which is when her right arm slides into her pocket and pulls out her knife to place it in his hand behind the chair.

She pulls back and looks at Lillian. "With him, we can still do this. He has the footage and the knowledge. Let John get a running head start, but he can't outrun what we've already planted."

"David," John interjects, "everything I promised you was the truth. No bullshit. You know you won't find what you're looking for here. Neither of us will. Help me, not them."

The tightness around his body loosens as the tape opens halfway. He applies pressure against it to help her saw through without giving away her movement. He feels awful that John believes he is a person capable of going along with something so dark, but he will have time to explain if they aren't murdered.

"This is my home, John," Lillian says. Her expression exudes a sorrow that grips David's chest.

"It's already dead, Lillian," John spits. "You're harvesting corpses."

Her sorrow contorts into anger, face flushing, nostrils flaring. She thrusts the knife forward and stabs him through the throat. Kyra drops the pocketknife onto David's lap and tackles Lillian to the ground. David leans forward, and the pressure tears the tape apart. He uses the knife to cut through the tape around his legs, keeping an eye on Kyra as she wrestles Lillian's knife out of her hands.

A stream of blood splatters onto the chair between his legs. He looks up to see John, wide-eyed, gurgling blood. David cuts through the tape and takes off his shirt to hold against John's throat with one hand while he cuts through the tape around John's wrists with the other. David waits for John to grab the shirt and then turns towards Lillian and Kyra, knife in front of his body, ready to threaten the older woman.

Lillian stands and pushes him away hard enough that he must reach a hand behind him and brace against the wall. She lunges at him with her knife in the air, ready to come down. He ducks out of the way and then runs towards Kyra, kneeling at her side. She holds her hands against her waist and opens her mouth as if to scream but only releases a whimper. Blood flows from beneath her hands. David's instinct is to apply pressure, but Lillian is already bounding across the room.

Instead of bracing to get out of the way, he turns and readies his body to lunge forward and meet her halfway, hoping to collide with her before her knife swings. John saves him from the risk by throwing his body forward, along with the chair still attached to his legs, and tackling Lillian back against the wall. David wraps his arm around Kyra's back and helps her off the floor.

"Lillian," Kyra strains to say.

"We need to get you to an ambulance." He doesn't have time to explain to her how he has been recording his own feeds in the communications room. "If we get away from her, we can explain everything. She's done."

She slips one bloodied hand away and pushed against the floor, helping David lift her to her feet. They make their way out of the door as John tries his best to keep Lillian on the ground, blood from his neck cascading onto her face and disorienting her. David stops. John might bleed out before they can get help, or Lillian might overpower him.

"Go," John croaks. "Help her."

That's all the motivation he needs. He helps Kyra through the door and down the hall. Ryan walks into the hallway from the stairway.

"Call for one of the ambulances," David yells, then remembers the multiple costumed people who were blocking his escape on the trail. Before he can react, Ryan grabs him by the neck with one hand and pushes Kyra with the other. Kyra screams as she hits the wall and drops to the floor. Ryan pins David against the wall opposite the stairway and uses both hands to tighten his grip.

David claws at Ryan's hands as blood rushes to his head and his vision blurs. He feels Ryan's face brush intimately close to his and then hears his voice whisper, "This is how I killed Dougie."

David screams against the pain, takes his hands from Ryan's and shoves both of his thumbs into Ryan's eye sockets. Ryan backs up and grabs his face. David pushes off the wall and kicks the other man in the chest. Ryan's body disappears down the dark stairway, and although David can't see the bottom, the thud, along with the scream's sudden halt, tells him they are free to move. He leans over to help Kyra back up and notices the paleness of her skin and closing eyelids. Her hands are still over her bleeding wound, but they are no longer applying pressure.

"Stay with me, Kyra," he despairs, lifting her arm over his shoulder and helping her stand. He knows that moving her is risky, but he doesn't know if Lillian will find her or one of her co-conspirators before he can retrieve help. If any co-conspirators remain, and which, if any, are knowledgeable about her murderous intentions, instead of blackmail. Not knowing how many people are involved with her plan will make their escape more treacherous.

They fumble down the stairs and over Ryan's body. David doesn't know if he killed the other man but knows now is not the time to dwell on the possibility. They leave the house and stumble down the hill. From the high vantage point, David sees more firefighters and ambulances pulling into the parking lot and snaking through the hayride's trail to get into the forest.

A mass of patrons squeezes through the main gate to exit while the fairground workers either help them or rush towards the corn, presumably to help with the fire that continues to spread to the surrounding forest. As they reach the bottom of the hill, the front door of the house bursts open. Lillian steps onto the porch and looks around, panting.

David pulls Kyra forward, but she is growing weaker by the minute. He could follow the trail north around the corn to get to the ambulances, but Lillian would be able to catch up to them. Instead, he heads through the corn. He can either try to hide in there as he snakes through to the other side, or head straight into the maze in hopes of losing her as they escape through to the other side.

"David!" Lillian screams as he crosses the path in front of the house and heads into the corn. He pushes them through the stalks until he emerges on the east side of the maze. Luckily, the design has never changed, so he knows exactly where to go.

"I can't, David," Kyra whispers. He wants to encourage her, but her head is limp, and her eyes are mere slits.

"Okay," he relents as he carries her to the closest stalk grouping that creates one of the interior walls. "Stay hidden here, and I'll draw her away." He sits her in the middle and uses a few husks to push against her wound. "Stay with me, okay? I'll bring help."

"David," she whispers. "I'm so sorry."

He wants to tell her she has nothing to be sorry about, but that would be disingenuous. "Save your apologies for when we are safe."

He backs out into the maze and sees the top of the stalks sway. He runs to the north end of the natural corridor and waits until he sees Lillian step inside.

"You won't get away with this, Lillian." He turns around the bend just in time for her to see him retreat. He runs forward, knowing the next right will split into two, and the one on the left leads to another right turn that is a dead-end.

"I can't let you ruin this farm, David!" she screams.

"Looks like you did that all by yourself!" he taunts her, hoping she follows so he can ambush her at the dead-end, where one of the cameras has been placed. If people are still tuned in, someone might be able to see her attacking. He waits around the bend and listens to her shuffle closer.

He readies Kyra's knife and looks towards the wall of stalks to check that the camera is still on its stand. The little green light on top tells him it's still transmitting to the communications room. The shuffling stops. Several seconds pass before he starts to think she might be onto his plan. Searing pain erupts in his lower back. He screams and tries to move forward, but an arm wraps around his chest and holds him steady.

"You think I don't know my own farm?" Lillian snarls, driving the knife deeper into his back. She releases his body, and he screams as he falls face-first to the dirt. The pain continues as she pulls the knife out of his back, causing him to scream again.

She grabs his arm and rolls him over, then straddles his waist, causing excruciating pressure on the wound in his back.

"I think," David talks through the pain, "your plan isn't going to work."

She pushes the blade against his neck. "You're the only loose end here."

"What about the others? Who else knows that you are going to blame John for the fire?"

"Nice try, David." For the first time, Lillian's desperate facade breaks. She looks at the camera. "I smashed your laptop and unplugged the feeds the second you left the shed," she says.

David's body chills, and although fear has been a part of him all night, for the first time since his father's verdict, he feels a complete loss of hope.

"I'm sorry it has to be this way, David," she whispers. "I'll tell them you died protecting me from John. At least your legacy will be better than your father's."

She adds pressure to the knife, and David closes his eyes. He is too weak to fight back, in body and spirit, so he braces for the blade to pierce through his skin. Instead, the pressure of Lillian's body around his waist lessens. He opens his eyes to see her fall next to him, her eyes closed. A line of blood drips from her hairline then down her temple.

"Did I just kill her?" Tracy stands above him holding a splintered piece of wood, her eyes wide with surprise. David doesn't think so but doesn't know how many words he will be able to speak with so much pain crawling up his back. He lifts a hand, and Tracy helps him stand slowly.

"Get a medic and bring them back. Kyra is hiding in here. She's almost bled to death."

Tracy nods and then turns towards the cornstalks.

"Wait," David croaks. "How did you know I was here?"

"Your Friend Finder is still on from the other night," she says, and then rushes through the stalks.

David walks from the dead-end, the pain in his right side causing him to limp.

"David," he hears a voice call from behind. Fear turns him around to see Lillian sitting on the ground, blood from her temple washing over John's dried blood down her face.

"Lillian," he answers.

"I just wanted to do what my parents did, and their parents before that. I didn't want their legacy to die because I wasn't good enough."

David remembers his father explaining that even though he couldn't forgive Eric for lying, he could understand his actions. Life is fucking difficult and weird.

"It's not your fault. Times change. People change. Things get harder. If it didn't happen during your life, it might have happened to whoever you left it to. I mean, you saw the end coming, and you tried to save it, so much so that you committed murder."

Lillian laughs without humor. "Thanks, David. I hope they know I tried my best."

"There's still—" he says but stops speaking as Lillian lifts the knife and stabs the blade into her neck. "No!" He screams and steps forward, but the pain sends him to the ground. Lillian's body teeters over and drops limply onto the ground. Her eyes stare up at the night sky as her blood drains into her family's soil.

MEDICS LIFT KYRA INTO the back of an ambulance. Her eyes are closed, and she is still deathly pale, but her chest is inflating and deflating.

"She'll be okay," Tracy offers, holding onto his hand at the back of their ambulance. He looks up and offers a smile.

"She's not who I'm concerned about."

"You'll be fine," Tracy says with a hint of playfulness. She leans back to look at the stitches the medic is sewing into his skin. "It looks worse than it is."

"It stabbed into your muscle, but it'll heal" the medic clarifies.

"It only stabbed into your muscle," Tracy repeats. "It'll heal."

"It's not that," he laments. He pulls out his phone and opens the live feed. "Lillian disconnected all the cameras. Without her direct confession…" he trails off as he sees Pam and Kevin sitting on the steps of the Ferris Wheel.

Their faces are covered with ash, and their costumes are tattered. Mark emerges from the stalks to the east, also in the robe without a mask. The medics carried two body bags out of the house. John and Ryan, he presumes. How many of them were in on the plan to frame John? Who only knew about the accident, and not the murderous lengths Lillian went to secure the farm's future? How many would have been complicit?

"The next few months are going to be a shit-show," Tracy finishes the thought for him. Having seen what he had gone through with his father, she knows how long the process will take and how it might not turn out in their favor. David killed a person, and he may have to face the consequences for that, even if he can prove it was in self-defense.

"Oh my God, David." His mother appears beyond the ring of police officers holding onlookers and reporters at bay. She tells a cop who stops her, "That's my son." He allows her inside. She picks up Ethan and carries him across the middle of the fairway.

"I'm okay, I'm okay," he assures his mother as she approaches the ambulance. "It only stabbed into my muscle. It'll heal."

Ethan rests his head in his mother's neck, reluctant to take his eyes from his brother.

"I'm okay, little man, I promise. She made it numb, so I don't even feel it."

Ethan nods his head but doesn't look up. His mother places her hand on Tracy's arm and says, "Thank you for saving my son."

"It was my pleasure," she says, patting David's curly hair like a dog.

"Hey, I did a lot of—" a question hits him in his mind like a bullet shot into his brain.

"How do you know that?" he asks his mother.

"How do I know what?" his mother asks.

"How do you know she saved me? You just got here."

His mother looks confused. "It was broadcast online. A lot of people saw it."

He pulls out his phone again and instead of opening his app, he goes to the public site and logs in. Each camera he clicks on is black.

"No, no one saw it after she unplugged it..." A thought occurs to him, and the implication fills him with a small amount of excitement. Hope.

"Were you watching on my computer?"

His mother looks at Ethan. He lifts his head and tells David, "Mom said I could."

"Lillian must have unplugged the monitors, not the receiver box." His eyes alight. "My transmitter is plugged into that, which is why..." The light dies in his eyes, and all hope drains from his heart. "You are the only ones who saw it."

Everyone goes quiet until the doctor declares that his stitches are complete.

"Do you want to watch it again?" Ethan asks.

"I wish I could, big guy. More than you know."

"We'll get through this," his mother says. She also knows the shit-show about to come.

"Why can't you?" Ethan asks.

"It was live. Happening in real-time. You can't go back."

"I saved it," he says.

David looks at him. "What do you mean?"

"I saved it when we started watching it."

David looks at his mother, then Tracy, and then back at Ethan. "You recorded everything you were watching?"

"Yeah," he says, his voice wavering now that everyone is looking at him. "You said it was like being in a real movie, so I thought you would want to watch it again." He tilts his head back into his mother's neck as though he has done something wrong.

"It's okay, Ethan; that is a great idea, but how did you record it?" David does not want hope to return if there isn't any hope. The feed had no record feature, so his brother must be confused about what he did.

"I went into the applications folder and clicked the screen recording button."

"How did you know how to do that?"

"Dad showed me on his computer last year when we were watching the Disney Halloween Parade."

"So, you recorded the whole thing?"

Ethan's face scrunches in worry. "Am I in trouble?"

David smiles, and hope fills his chest so much that for the first time in a year, his stomach unclenches.

"No, Ethan," he laughs. "You are the opposite of in trouble. You just saved Halloween."

"I did?" Ethan picks his head back up.

"Yeah, buddy. You are the new Pumpkin King."

Epilogue

October 31st

Wesley doesn't understand the appeal of Halloween. As a kid, he rolled his eyes when his older brothers tried to use rubber masks and hide plastic spiders in his bed to scare him. One time, when their parents weren't home, they used a Ouija board to try to scare him, and he pretended to be scared because he knew that's what his older brothers wanted, and if they didn't get it, they might escalate their torture. Nothing about Halloween, from scary movies to creepy crawlies, ever created a single goosebump on his skin.

The monstrous house in front of him is no exception, especially since he's been through it over a dozen times before. His brothers always thought the farm's attractions were a blast at Halloween, but he only wanted to come for the s'mores and apple cider. He was also a crack shot at the darts and pellet-gun booths. His brothers collected memories at the farm, but Wesley collected prizes. But the prizes have not aged with him, and so the victory is short-lived. Had he been able to time-travel to tell his younger self he would be attending the Halloween attraction at Badger's Farm, he is sure that little boy would have called him "lame."

Nothing at the farm can scare Wesley, and the only prize he is there for is the petite blonde, grabbing his wrist and leading him towards the "Reaper's House." Alisha stops at the back of the line and stands on the tips of her shoes to see one of the "Reapers" ushering the patrons inside, five at a time, pointing with a plastic scythe. Wesley wraps his arms around her waist and leans down to kiss her neck, giving her skin a playful nip between his teeth.

"Someone's excited," she says, baring her neck for him to continue.

"Excited to get you out of here," he says, and kisses her neck again.

"I need to get scared first, then you can do whatever you want."

"Oh, so you like the danger?"

"Mmhmm," she says, and pushes her ass into his crotch.

"Well, you definitely picked the right place."

She turns around and wraps her arms around his neck. "You've been here before?"

"When I was a kid," he shrugs, "but I mean with what happened here last year."

Her eyes widen, and her arms tighten, drawing her body closer. "What happened?"

He is surprised she hasn't heard about the case, but since her dating profile says she lives in Philly, it's possible the news hasn't been picked up outside of Jersey. That will change once the Netflix documentary drops, he figures.

"Two years ago, on Halloween, the farm's owner killed a bunch of people and then set fire to one of the attractions."

"Which attraction?" Her eyes widen even more, their irises a shining blue that makes him weak in his knees... and stronger in other places.

"I think it was one of the hayride stops. They found the bodies of her victims there and more in her house," he nods towards the looming house on the hill to the north. Alisha glances over her shoulder at it and then back at Wesley.

"More," she hisses.

Wesley laughs but is wary of her obsession with horror. When she pinged him on the dating site, he read her profile, which detailed that she loved everything horror-related, books, movies, and true-crime podcasts. He considered those details trite, even ordinary. Every twenty-something likes true crime podcasts. However, this girl seems to be getting off on it. He's never been on a date where he considers the possibility he'll awaken in a bathtub without any kidneys in the morning, but there is a first for everything. Perhaps that's why her first message on the app sounded too eager to meet him.

"A few people who worked here went to trial for it," he tries to remember the details. "Some for being part of a conspiracy to commit fraud, and at least one who knew about the murders. The guy who uncovered it made a documentary that's coming out on Netflix on Friday. It took over a year to rebuild, which is why this is only open for one night only."

"You should come over and watch it with me," she says, and kisses him deeply. Obsessed or not, he has never had a date as hot or as interested in him as Alisha. He laughs internally, realizing that if he did watch the documentary with her, she might actually want to watch it, rather than "Netflix and Chill."

Someone clears their throat behind them to tell them the line is moving, but she doesn't stop kissing him. He wraps his arms around her waist and picks her up to close the distance between them and the people ahead in line. He wants nothing more than this silly shit to be over with, so he decides to shoot his shot.

"How hot would it be to have our first time be in the place where they found the bodies? Maybe we should sneak away to find it?" he offers. He wonders whether telling her about his secrets would turn her on even more or make her run. The bubbly expression she has worn since seeing her for the first time drops, and her voice loses humor.

"Scary foreplay, first. Then, I'm going to terrify you with what my body can do." She places her long red fingernail under his chin and gives it a playful scratch. The smile that returns is more sinister than seductive.

There go my kidneys.

The reaper opens the door and points the plastic scythe inside, ushering in the group ahead. A few seconds later, it motions for Alisha and him to enter. A raspy voice behind the rubber mask tells them to "Choose your fate" as they enter.

Despite not being interested in Halloween shenanigans, the macabre scene in the atrium is an impressive spectacle. The room is awash in wavering blue light, creating the illusion of being submerged in water. From the domed ceiling hang mannequin mermaids sculpted and painted with such detail that they seem real. They reach clawed, bloodied talons downward at him and bare razor-sharp teeth underneath hunger-filled scowls. The surrounding walls, curving stairway, and second-floor banister are adorned with rotting corpses wearing bathing suits and skeleton remains of pirates and sea captains.

"Where did they get the budget?" he hears someone echo his thought from within the group of three ahead. They are moving around the stairs and heading into a hallway whose entrance is decorated to resemble a cave mouth, complete with starfish, conch shells, and bones wearing tattered clothes.

"Let's go up first," Alisha says, once again grabbing his wrist and leading him up the stairs like a child. He doesn't protest. The quicker they get through this, the quicker he can get under Alisha's little black dress.

The long, exhausting stairs end with a thin balcony where the only way forward is through a hallway illuminated by aquamarine light emanating up from the Plexiglas flooring. Inside is a bedding of coral reef, decorated with fake sea anemones, shells, eels, piranhas, and rotting corpses. Something soft brushes against Wesley's forehead and makes him gasp. He looks up to see the edges of bloodied and tattered clothes, jewelry, and beach towels.

"Lame," he scoffs to hide the embarrassment of being surprised.

"You're lame," Alisha says, but her voice doesn't sound playful. She moves ahead until all he can see of her are thin spills of light across her pale legs, until she disappears into the darkness ahead.

"Where are you going?" he calls but receives no reply. He is about to call her name when he is startled by a crash to his left. Something grabs his shirt and pulls him towards the wall, then he feels arms hook under his armpits and lift his body upwards.

Before he can struggle against the grip, his body is pulled over an edge and then released. He falls and hits the floor hard enough to push all the air out of his lungs. He gasps for air as something grabs the collar on the back of his neck and thrusts him forward. His body rolls across hardwood until it hits a wall.

"What the..." he tries to say, but still does not have enough air to speak.

"Happy Halloween, Wesley." The use of his name compels him to look up at the reaper above. He doesn't recognize the person through the manipulated deep voice they are speaking with, nor can he tell if it is a man or a woman. He coughs and clears his throat.

"How do you know my name?"

"I know a lot about you, Wesley Banks. The question is, what can you tell me?" The reaper moves its scythe around and jams it underneath Wesley's chin to push up on his neck. He feels pain erupt and blood trickle down his neck. The reaper traded the plastic scythe for the real tool. It lifts him to his knees.

"What do you want to know?" he asks, but he has a hint of the nature of this attack. This isn't the first time he's been threatened because of his work, but since that first time, he has been able to get away with anything, everything, through anonymity. He doesn't know how this person found him through his aliases, but he will need to wipe his hard drives and rebuild his hardware and software from scratch. Again.

"Four years ago, you were contacted about changing insurance paperwork and forging a name."

"I don't know what you're talking about," he says, trying not to cry from the pain. The blade rises, pushing deeper into his skin. He hears blood dripping onto the floor. The pain forces out a cry along with a bout of honesty.

"Fine, fine. Yes, I remember something like that. I can fix it. Is that what you want?"

"What you did helped a murderer frame and kill an innocent man. What's done is done. Right now, there is another innocent man imprisoned because of you. You doctored emails to make him look negligent at his job, which got another man killed."

"I do a lot of hacking, a lot of doctoring for a lot of people."

The reaper adds pressure to the blade and nearly digs into his throat. Wesley searches his memory but doesn't need long to recall the name. He typically avoids the aftermath of his gigs as much as possible to avoid absorbing too much guilt, but the trial was reported on every news station in the tri-state area.

"Lucas Earhart," he says.

The blade digs deeper.

"What do you want me to do?"

The reaper speaks slowly, purposefully, emphasizing every word when it says, "You can confess."

"This is my livelihood," he cries.

"You took another's livelihood away," the reaper says. "Separated him from his family."

"I know, I know. I'm sorry."

"Tell me," the reaper demands.

"The guy's boss paid me to change the emails to look like the roles were reversed, then erase the email the boss sent telling Earhart he should still use the equipment. I made it look like Earhart was ignoring the boss, not the other way around."

The reaper lowers the scythe. Wesley leans forward and grabs his bloody neck.

"I won't do it," he says. "You can threaten me all you want, but I won't confess."

Wesley's skin grows cold as the reaper remains silent for longer than he can take it. He looks up and sees the scythe lifted into the air. He braces himself for death, resigned not to scream. At least his wife will collect some insurance money after his death. But death does not come.

The reaper points with the scythe towards the ceiling in the same manner it had ushered him inside the house. Hanging there is a digital camera with a red recording light.

"You already have."

ACKNOWLEDGMENTS

My heart is full of thanks to Candace Nola, who published this book. She believes in my writing and inspires me to grow with every word. You are a treasure, Candace.

Special thanks to Grant McSurdy, for his encouragement and for being my champion beta reader. If he hadn't liked this story, it wouldn't have been completed.

Thanks to my family and friends for their love and support, and for putting up with how much I love Halloween.

To you. Writing stories means nothing if no one is eager to read. I hope you enjoyed this Halloween celebration.

—Patrick Tumblety 2025

About the Author

Patrick Tumblety is an author of horror, science fiction, and poetry. He has been featured in numerous anthologies, including **Tales of Jack the Ripper** from Word Horde Press, **The Dead Inside** from Dark Dispatch, and **Sincerely, Departed**, created by Cat Voleur and Angel Krause.

His first horror novel, **Come Out & Play**, debuted in September 2024 from Uncomfortably Dark Horror and has been reviewed as *"A poignant look at how our trauma bleeds into every part of our lives. My heart didn't know whether to break or race."* (Laurel Hightower, Bram Stoker Nominated Author).

Patrick lives in Delaware with his wife, daughter, and their cat, Mittens, where he spends his time writing, playing video games, and teaching self-defense to those who want to be prepared for all the monsters that may come.

ANTHOLOGIES
Uncomfortably Dark presents The Baker's Dozen-2021 Dark Dozen anthology & the 2022 Splatterpunk award-winning extreme horror anthology.

Uncomfortably Dark presents Trapped-2022 Dark Dozen anthology that explores themes of horror focused on being trapped in an unspeakable situation.

Uncomfortably Dark presents Dark Disasters-2023 Dark Dozen anthology that explores horrific situations unfolding during natural disasters.

Uncomfortably Dark presents Full Throttle-2025 Dark Dozen Anthology that is a full-blown extreme horror anthology dedicated to survivors of sexual violence.
This anthology contains no scenes of sexual violence.

The Generator-quad collaboration anthology featuring Candace Nola, Eric Butler, M Ennenbach, and Nikolas P. Robinson.

Dark Disturbances- 2024 Uncomfortably Dark Author Sampler Anthology.

Dark Asylum – 2025 Uncomfortably Dark Author Sampler
Anthology.

<u>NOVELS & COLLECTIONS</u>
EPISODES OF VIOLENCE by David Bernstein
DREAMWHISPERS by M Ennenbach
CREMATED REMAINS by M Ennenbach
CUCKOO by M Ennenbach
OLD TOO SOON by Brian Bowyer
BLACKOUT: MICROPOETRY by Brian Bowyer
INNOCENCE ENDS by Nikolas P. Robinson
HAVE A BLAST by Nikolas P. Robinson
COME OUT & PLAY by Patrick Tumblety
ROADS TO RUIN by Brian Bowyer
SUBJECT A by M Ennenbach
OIOS LYKOS by M Ennenbach
STORYSLAVE by Brian Bowyer
VERUM MALUM by Michael R. Collins
PENNYROYAL TEA by Aaron Lebold
THE SHERIFF OF SALEM by Aaron Lebold
GENOCIDE by Aaron Lebold
QUARANTINE by Aaron Lebold
BLASPHEMY by Aaron Lebold
SLENDER BONES IN SACRED SOIL by Fredrick Niles
THIS IS HOW A VILLAIN IS MADE by Amanda Headlee
COFFEE SHOP by Aaron Lebold

**Order signed copies and limited-edition hardcovers from
the shop:**
https://www.uncomfortablydark.com/shop

Join our Patreon for free books, merch, and more!
https://www.patreon.com/user/membership?u=12231330&view
_as=patron